The Secret Mission of Princess Camille

J. C. Pressman

The Secret Mission of Princess Camille

Published by Wheatmark™
610 East Delano Street, Suite 104
Tucson, Arizona 85705 U.S.A.
www.wheatmark.com
International Standard Book Number: 978-1-58736-843-1
Library of Congress Control Number: 2007925279

Doll on the front cover provided by the dolls' store of Molly Kate, Andover, MA.

Part One

Chapter 1

It was a beautiful morning. The sun just peeking over the horizon, sent shafts of light into the eastern sky. In just one hour, heat and increased humidity would send people scurrying for shade, but for the moment all was calm, except that is for the sound of birds on a distant rim; hundreds of them on the cliffs edge, wheeling and diving into the valley below.

From the silhouette of the city, the silence was broken by the occasional sound of a truck motor as it crested a hill, its lights twinkling as it bounced from side to side on the uneven surface of the road. All that was left as it descended out of sight and sound was a cloud of black smoke which hung close to the road in the morning air.

After some time, the truck arrived on the open patch of ground and headed towards the cliff. The engine roared with each gear change, accompanied by puffs of black smoke shooting into the air above the cab. Brakes were applied and a continuous squeal sent birds soaring as it pierced the morning air. The driver, a small heavy set man with black curly hair poking out from under a tattered old cap, stuck his arm out of the window; he was wearing a ragged tee shirt with the sleeves missing. He opened the door and leaned out, looking rearward as he put the truck in reverse and made a wide arc towards the cliff. Again the squealing of brakes; the truck stopped right at the lip, and the driver revved up the engine. The bed of the truck shook along its whole length and slowly lifted up into the air on the front end. The doors at the rear of the truck swung open and the contents slithered out into the darkness below. The truck shook and shuddered as the driver forced the bed to rise to its maximum height ensuring that none of its contents had remained in the bed. Then, with the sound of air escaping, the bed slowly returned to its normal position and the rear doors clanged shut. The driver ground the engine into first gear and moved off, changing gears as he bounced from side to side along the road. Slowly the sound began to ebb and he disappeared into the haze toward the city. From out of this haze came another truck similar to the first, bouncing along the same road towards the cliff. This passing of trucks, one returning empty of cargo, the other fully laden, set the pattern for the day.

The sun had risen in the sky and it was now easier to see birds swooping down onto the huge mound of rubble below. There were plastic bottles, cans, clothing and paper everywhere. Cardboard boxes, tires; it just piled up as far as the eye could see, all lying along side partially consumed fruit and vegetables and articles of clothing. Close to the bottom of the pile, heavier articles such as chairs, sofas, pipes of all sizes, bath tubs and large pieces of machinery had rolled down the steep slope and settled next to strands of wire and paper at the bottom. Paper, which had not become dampened by rotting food and oil, fluttered in the updraft.

Quite suddenly large black rats, it seemed like hundreds, emerged from beneath the piles of rubble. They ran and jumped over each other, squealing as they climbed the mounds of rubbish searching for pieces of food and rotting vegetation, anything in fact that could be eaten. So numerous were they that the whole mountain of rubble appeared to move.

From an outcropping of rocks a short distance away from the bottom of the pile, there was some movement. A piece of corrugated sheeting clattered as it fell to the ground. Something emerged from the rock opening in the gray light of dawn; its movement was slow and ponderous as it escaped the dark shadows made by the rocks. Slowly the form came into focus. There at the bottom of the heap, completely alone, stood a little girl about six years old. She had short dark hair and large black eyes sunken into her gaunt face. She wore a little pink ragged dress which finished at about the knees. The little girl was standing on one leg leaning on a crutch which was under her left arm. She hobbled, quite quickly towards the pile of rubble, stopping at its base. A partially eaten apple, had rolled down the hill, and lay at her feet. She stooped to picked it up, scarcely glancing at the fruit as she bit into it. Wielding the crutch expertly, she moved paper aside as she dug into the pile. After a few seconds of rummaging, she found half of a cucumber which she picked up, rubbing it against her dress before eating it.

Looking up and along the pile for food of some kind, something caught her eye; something so completely out of place in this pile of refuse and rotting food from the city that she just stared and pondered what it could be. It appeared to be a large roll of beautiful white, lace like material, about 80 centimeters long, resting against a worn truck tire just out of reach. It was certainly an unusual sight for it stood out white and clean against the pile of rubble upon which it rested.

The little girl threw herself onto the pile and started clawing her way up it with both hands, at the same time digging in with her one good leg. Finally, she was able to grab the tire and pull it away from the heap. The roll tumbled into the place left by the tire. She continued her way up the heap inch by inch until she was able to grasped the end of the roll and pull it towards her. She clasped the bundle under her arm, and turning onto her back, slid to the bottom of the heap.

The crutch had become hidden under some of the trash displaced by her arms and leg as she had clawed her way to the bundle. Feverously she searched for it, occasionally glancing over her shoulder along the trail which led to the forest. She felt under the rubble, and breathed a sigh of relief as her hand made contact with it. The bottom of the heap was always wet, so the crutch slid in her hand as she removed it from its slimy grave. She ran her hand down its length to remove some paper wrapped around it, and then she reached down for the bundle and tucked it under her arm. With the aid of the crutch she pulled herself to her feet and quickly shuffled off towards the entrance to her cave.

In the distance a crowd of people were running toward the pile as more refuse fell down the hill as it discharged from a truck above. Quickly she entered the cave, laid her bundle down and lifted the heavy corrugated iron door into the recess. Shafts of sunlight penetrated her home through pieces of broken glass that Alfredo had carefully cut to take the form of the openings. These served both as windows and protection from rats and the Monsoons. The cave was quite small, though high enough for her to stand upright and still leave some space above her head. Opposite the entrance against the far wall was a pile of rags which served as her bed. It was here that she kneeled, near her pillow, and moved the rags away until the bare earth appeared below. Brushing away a layer of earth with her hands, she uncovered a wooden board. She removed the board, and under it was an opening which let into the cave wall. It wasn't a very large opening but wide enough for a small body to crawl into, and it was quite deep. She pushed her precious bundle of white lace into the hole and put the board back over it, scooping back some earth until the board was partially covered. Finally she arranged her bedding over it.

There was sound of movement at the cave entrance. Her heart started to pound. Someone on the outside was calling her name. "Lillianna! Are you there?".It was her friend Maria. Maria was a woman in her mid thirties. She was slim and her hands were rough and worn through years of toil keeping her family clean and fed, but her face was soft and gentile and she always able to smile no matter what the problem was that confronted her. She had met Lillianna's mother, very briefly and under tragic circumstances, when early one morning, six years earlier, she had heard a strange noise on the porch of her hut. A woman carrying a baby under one arm had crawled up the stairs to Maria's home before collapsing in front of the door. Maria had run to her and sank to her knees to cradle the woman in her arms. The baby was lying at her mother's side covered in blood and had a piece of cloth tied like a tourniquet around one badly broken leg. Her last words to Maria, gasping in her dying breath were. "My name is Camille, and this is my daughter Lillianna. I beg of you to take care of her!" The mother died still looking up into Maria's tearful eyes. Maria had run, with the baby in her arms, to the visiting first aid wagon, which by sheer fortune, happened to be in the village that day. The nurse and her assistant took one look at the baby's wounds, jumped into the wagon and drove with the baby at high speed back toward town.

It was about two months later that the wagon returned with the baby inside. Maria hadn't really expected to see the baby again, and was shocked to see that its left leg had been removed to just above the knee. It had been due to Maria's quick action, and the fact that the visiting nurse and her assistant just happened to be in the neighborhood, that the baby's life had been saved.

True to her word, Maria took the baby and raised her as her own, along with her three other children. It had been extremely difficult, and when Lillianna was big enough, she had moved out to be closer to the dump. At first the family refused to let her go, but Lillianna would leave when all were asleep in the middle of the night, and they would find her sleeping near the heap in the morning. Although she had been bitten a few times by rats she continued to go there. It was then that Alfredo had discovered the cave and had closed it off with a corrugated iron door that he had fashioned. He had added windows where there were cracks in the rock open to the sky above. He had made it a safe refuge from rats, and bragged that even Mosquitoes would not be able to enter when the door was closed. From then on, if she did run away at night she would be safe and secure.

Gradually over the months, the family got used to Lilianna's running away to be close to the food pile in the morning. It was horrible living so close to that awful smell with only rats for companions, but she enjoyed her independence and felt much less of a burden to her family in their crowded home. She was always the first at the pile in the morning and first to take scraps of food that fell from the trucks.

"I'm coming Maria." she said, taking her crutch and walking towards the door. "Please don't wait for me; you will miss your food!"

Maria's husband Alfredo was already at the pile with his sack. He left his wife and daughters to collect food, while he searched for wood to make a fire, or for pieces of metal that he could make into something to sell at the Market in town. He was a clever man and could make or repair almost anything. He loved his family and always tried to make their lives as easy as possible working long and hard whenever he was able, never giving thought to his health or the hunger pains that tore into him at the end of a long days work; and through it all, he always endeavored to enter the door of his home with a big grin on his face.

Lillianna emerged from her home in the rocks and Maria ran to greet her. They hugged each other, and Maria ran her hand through Lillianna's hair. Lillianna was glad to feel Maria's body close to hers and hugged her tightly.

"Lillianna my precious, I think that we should go and wash our clothes and ourselves in our home this afternoon." Lillianna looked up at her smiling.

"Yes. I would like to do that, I've collected enough soap." They walked slowly back to the pile.

A few men could be seen picking up empty cans and metal objects. Occasionally they would reach down and take some morsel of food, a few segments of an orange, a carrot or half eaten apple, but for the most part they foraged for items that would be of some use to them back at the camp. Food collecting was the work of women and children. It was also their task to find clothing for the family. The pile was now alive with people and the rats had disappeared to the safety of their dens.

Some of the older boys were waiting near the top for the next truck to arrive. When it came, it was their job to find items of value and throw them down to a family member waiting below. Sometimes a fight would break out as a package intended for one family was intercepted by another, but these were infrequent and for the moment all was calm. Maria waved to Lillianna. She had her sack fully laden with food products and slowly descended the slope to the ground.

"Come, my precious. It's time for us to return. We have

enough food for two days and you must eat with us." Lillianna had also gathered enough food for herself to eat for two days. Tomorrow would be Sunday and there would be no trucks. Today was always a good day for food, as yesterday had been market day in town and often perishable items were thrown away and collected by the trash men in the evening, who hauled them to the dump the following morning.

Maria was joined by her younger daughter Sandra, who was about the same age as Lillianna. She walked over to Lillianna and squeezed her around the waist at the same time kissing her on the cheek.

"How are you doing today, all alone in that little cave of yours?"

"I'm ok, I suppose. Your father has made it really comfortable for me there".

"No more rats?"

"No more rats! The door works well, and it is always cooler in there"

"Good, but let's go back to my place now Lillie." Sandra had beautiful long dark hair and resembled her mother. She waited while Lillianna adjusted the crutch under her arm.

"Ok my Sandrino, but first I need to drop this food off and pick up some clothing and my soap; you just won't believe how much soap I have!"

The girls walked into the cave, emerging soon after with packages in their hands. Lillianna pulled back on the corrugated piece of iron which served as a door. It was heavy, but when closed it was a perfect fit in the rock face thanks to the work done by Sandra's father with the help of his son Pedro. Pedro was about fourteen years old and very handsome. He looked like his father but had his mother's soft eyes. Lillianna liked him a lot but then so did many other girls, and he was practically a man, and she was to him, just a little girl whom he teased and treated like his little sister.

Sandra picked up the bag of clothes and the soap which Lillianna had saved, and started down the road towards the camp. They passed through a grove of bamboo trees on a path worn by many years of use. One could see the work of the woodman's axe at the sides of the road; nothing new would be allowed to take hold here, but beyond this on each side, thick masses of bamboo and vegetation flanked the pathway and closed in over their heads.

Soon they arrived at the camp. It was on a flat plain at the foot of a hill covered in bamboo and ferns. They could hear the sound of water as it flowed down hill through a series of falls to the village; it wound its way through the settlement and emptied into a small lake before returning once more to the jungle. It was because of this abundant supply of water and the close proximity of the dump, that the village had come into being. The food source, and items of clothing and furniture, however poor in quality, enabled the poor and destitute to survive.

There were over fifty huts of all shapes and sizes in the village, made from bamboo and anything that could be used from the dump. Bamboo was the common roof construction, but this would be replaced by sheets of corrugated iron and plywood as they became available. In this way it was fairly easy to see which huts had been there the longest. People waved from the doorway of their homes to

Lillianna as she came into view. Sandra's oldest sister Vivienne also stood in the entrance to her parent's house. She was slim and majestic like her mother, and was the oldest of the four children, one having arrived a year earlier. She was hardly a child though having reached the age of eighteen. She ran towards them as they approached, and took Lillianna into her arms.

"Lillianna my baby, you seem to have grown taller every time I see you." They embraced and walked towards the home, Lillianna moving swiftly with the crutch that Alfredo had fashioned for her.

Their house was the first one in the village and closest to the waterfall. During the monsoon periods, the stream became a torrent and the falls were at times, quite deafening, but at this moment and for most of the year it was in the best location. Alfredo and his family had lived there for many years, and had made it larger and more attractive as his means allowed. He had been lucky to get it from a friend who had found employment in the city. Like others in the area it was made of boards and sheets of metal, but it was softened by the plants and vines that grew up around it. Alfredo and Pedro had made a thatch of bamboo leaves to cover the corrugated metal roof. This helped protect the home from the suns penetrating heat, but more importantly it placed a barrier between the roof and rain during the monsoon seasons, without which the sound of torrential rain on the roof would have been deafening.

Alfredo had recently placed some bamboo pipes in the ground with their upper ends in the river, so that water flowed continuously through them into a stone basin in the kitchen and from there they overflowed into the monsoon ditch around his house and those of his neighbors. During the rainy season these ditches would be full of swiftly flowing water, and it was quite common to see drowned rats floating by. These rats were enormous and were the size of large cats. That season however, was still a few months away and for now the water trickled lazily between stones in the bottom of the hollow. They crossed the boards over the ditch and walked up the few stairs into the house.

Lillianna was happy to feel the familiar bamboo floor under her foot, and she was looking forward to her bath. Vivienne had already started to fill the large tub with water as it lay on the floor next to the sink. She turned towards Lillianna.

"Here my baby, give me your clothes and I will wash them while you take your bath." Lillianna removed a small piece of soap from her sack and hopped towards the tub. She leaned against the sink and removed all of her clothes. Her left leg had been cut just above the knee; the end had long since healed over, but seeing Lillianna's frail body and in that condition always brought lines of sadness to Vivienne's face, which she tried hard to conceal. She so wanted to squeeze Lillianna tightly and never let her go, but she knew that for Lillianna's sake it was best to hide her emotions. She picked Lillianna up and placed her in the tub.

"Where did you get this soap? It smells so good." said Vivienne holding the sliver to her nose. Lillianna laughed heartily.

"I found it in the pile. I've been very lucky lately."

Vivienne knelt by the tub and poured a jug of water

over Lillianna's head, then ran the soap over it until a good lather had formed. The smell of lavender filled the air. "Ok my baby. I'm going to let you wash yourself, while I wash your clothes at the sink.

Maria started the fire under the small iron grill placed on the ground over some charcoal at the back of the house, and it was from here that she saw Pedro returning from upstream where he had been fishing all morning. He had been successful and had returned to the village with several fish, some of which he had given to their neighbor who was always grateful as there were many children to feed in his home; but he still retained enough for his family. Alfredo had been working in town during the week and had gone to the market and bought some vegetables. It was these that Lillianna could smell cooking on the grill as she washed herself. They smelled so good. Maria was such a good cook and could make wonderful meals out of almost anything. Lillianna tried to ignore the hunger pains which were so much part of her life and concentrated on cleaning her face and arms.

Vivienne was singing at the sink and had wrung Lillianna's clothes out and laid them in the sun to dry. She continued to do more of the family's laundry. When Lillianna had finished washing herself she stood up in the tub so that Vivienne could pour clean water over her. Standing up was easy for her, but stepping out of the tub was almost impossible since the walls were high and she had nothing to hang onto. Vivienne lifted her out, and she hopped over to the window to dry herself off under the sun's rays.

Vivienne came towards Lillianna with a dress that she had made for Sandra a few years earlier. Even though she had added a hem to the dress, it was now too small for Sandra as she was growing broader across the shoulders.

"I want you to try this on my little flee. You should be big enough for it now." Lillianna eyes were large like saucers.

"Oh it's so pretty! I've always loved it so. I shall feel like a princess in it." She quickly slipped the dress on her back which was still wet. Tears came to her eyes. "It's so beautiful; will Sandra mind?" Vivienne reassured her that it was Sandra's idea.

"You are all so kind to me I don't know what would have become of me without you."

"If we are kind to you it's because you are part of our family and you must never forget it. We love you very much and wish you would return to us here where we can protect you."

Lillianna hopped over to Vivienne and put her arms around her.

"I will return one day I promise, when I get my new leg; but for now you have many mouths to feed and for me it's so much easier to live closer to the hill."

Maria entered the room with baby Anita in her arms. The baby had just woken up and was smiling at everyone. Her eyes were very large and black.

"May I hold her Maria?"

Lillianna hopped towards a stool in the corner of the room and sat down with her arms extended before her. "Of course you may my precious." Maria walked towards her. Lillianna took the baby, who was large and healthy and almost completely filled her lap.

"You are so big my baby." said Lillianna, as she kissed

her on each cheek and started to rock her in her arms as Maria left the room.

Maria came up the rough wooden steps into the kitchen. She was carrying a tray of food which was steaming hot. The odor filled the room and Lillianna started to swallow as her mouth began to fill with digestive juices. "Everyone come to the table. Girls wash your hands please!" she said as she placed the tray in the middle of the plastic plates, which were arranged neatly around the table. Utensils made of bamboo were at the side of each plate. There were chairs at each end fashioned from bamboo, and bamboo benches along both sides of the table. Maria left the room to pick up some more dishes of food, while the girls stood at the sink washing their hands.

Pedro ambled into the room and kissed Lillianna on the cheek. "Hi little sister." he yelled, as he took the baby in his hands and raised her over his head. "And you too baby Anita. Hi." Anita let out a few gurgles of joy. Lillianna looked at Pedro. He was tall and lean and very dark from the sun's rays. His teeth were a dazzling white. Lillianna felt a warm glow come to her cheeks.

"I'm not your sister!" she murmured under her breath before she realized it.

"Oh yes you are!" Pedro grunted, as he threw Anita into the air and caught her in his arms. It was then that Alfredo came from washing his hands and took the baby from Pedro.

"Everyone, come to the table!" said Alfredo, he was a quiet man, not given to many words, but when he spoke his words were taken seriously. Maria walked into the room with a roasted chicken and placed it at the end of the table next to Alfredo. Vivienne let out a cry of surprise.

"Lillianna, you must come more often!" Everyone laughed until Alfredo called for silence. Maria had seated herself at the other end of the Table.

"Let us join hands and bow our heads in prayer." he said. They all joined hands and bowed their heads as Alfredo spoke. "Lord we give thanks for the food which you have set before us and for our daughter Lillianna who has come to visit us. We pray that you will watch over us and keep us safe. Amen.".

Alfredo rose and taking the large knife laying on the side of the plate, skillfully cut the chicken into several portions, adding a piece to each of the plates as they were passed around the table. Maria moved around the table putting generous servings of vegetables on each dish. She took little for herself, leaving her food to concentrate on feeding Anita.

Chapter 2

It was 5.30 when Lillianna said goodbye to the family. She kissed and hugged each one avoiding Pedro until the last. He came over, picked her up and swung her around a couple of times before kissing her on each cheek and setting her down.

"Goodbye little sister and come back soon" he called out as she hopped towards the door. She took her crutch and placed the sack full of clean clothes, by the loops onto her shoulder. She waved and went down the steps onto the pathway. Tears welled up and ran down her cheeks, as she hobbled along the path through the jungle. She wiped her eyes with the back of her hand and took a few deep breaths. She had only ten minutes to walk to her home in the rocks but night fell quickly in these parts and it would be completely dark by seven. She had just over one hour of daylight left.

It was not until Lillianna was in her room with the

door pulled into its frame and bolted behind her that she remembered the package she had found that morning on the heap. First she would change to save her beautiful new dress from getting dirty. She emptied her sack putting the two plastic bottles of fresh water next to the empty ones in the corner beside the door. She put on her old pink dress. It smelled fresh and clean as it had dried by the afternoon sun's rays.

Lillianna went to her bed and removed some rags and dug down a little to the board in front of the opening. She tugged on the board until it came loose from the rock and then threw it behind her. Reaching down into the hole she pulled out the bundle. "What beautiful linen." she exclaimed as she ran her hands over it. Lillianna had never seen anything so pretty. "All that lace. It must have taken many people many days to make it!"

She moved the roll to the bottom of the bed and started to unroll it over the rags. It had been folded upon itself twice. Not only was it very long but also quite wide. She continued to unroll the package but ran out of bed space and was obliged to go the other way, and then back again for a third time. The sun had fallen behind the trees, and in the darkness of the cave she could no longer see very clearly, but she had become so excited at her find that she decided to light the candle that Alfredo had left for emergencies; and this surely was one. Her hands trembled as she struck the match head against the rock face. It sputtered into life and she quickly held it to the candle. A glow filled the darkness spreading out to the farthermost corners of the room. She put it in the niche in the wall just above the bed and quickly got back to her job of unrolling the linen. Finally it came to an end. There, to her absolute amazement, as she pulled back the last flap, she looked upon the most beautiful doll she had ever seen in her life. The doll's eyes were closed. She had real eyelashes, which Lillianna touched lightly with her finger hardly believing what she saw. Her long flaxen hair hung down disappearing behind a beautiful dress of lace. She picked the doll up and held her to her body as the words 'Mama' called out to her. She held the doll away from her and looked into dark blue eyes which were wide open. Her lashes were long and curved down onto her cheeks.

"Hello my baby." Don't be afraid, Mama has you." She pulled the doll into her arms and sobbed loudly." "Mama has you."

After some time in that position, she laid the doll down so that she could see her. The doll's dress was long, like that of a Princess. Lillianna lifted its dress. She had black shiny shoes and white stockings, which were attached to a garter belt around her waist. "Oh my little one, you have two beautiful legs. You really are a Princess! I have dreamed so often about being like you. I shall call you:.'The Princess Camille.' She picked her up and heard her say 'Mama' again. "You are safe now my darling, Mama won't let anything hurt you ever again." She pulled the doll close to her. "Come my baby, it is time for bed. Mama will be right beside you; but now we must sleep".

Lillianna pulled back a layer of linen and put the doll inside. She climbed in beside the doll, rising up to blow out the candle. In the darkness she pulled the doll next to her and held her in her arms. "No more loneliness." she whispered and kissed the doll on the cheek. She lay there for some time, the smell of clean linen around her and fumes from a spent candle in the air. Finally she sank into a deep and satisfying sleep.

During the night she dreamed many dreams, where she was running through the woods with baby Camille holding her hand; they were jumping over ferns and flowers. Birds of many colors were everywhere, and deer ran along the track ahead of them, occasionally looking back to see if they were following. They stopped to eat near a stream, where food was growing along its banks, and they drank from its cool clear waters. Contented and happy they lay in the soft green grass looking up through the canopy of trees to the cool blue sky above where birds swarmed chasing the afternoon sun.

When Lillianna awoke, the sun was already high in the sky, sending shafts of light through the two small windows in the roof of the cave. One fell almost directly upon the bed where she lay. She turned in the bed and saw light playing upon the flaxen hair of her baby. It seemed to bounce off her curls. Lillianna moved her head from side to side in disbelief. She sat up directly in bed and leaned against the rock.

"It's time to wake up my baby Camille!" She pulled her doll into the upright position and turned it towards her and kissed her on the cheek. The doll opened her eyes and said 'Mama'.

"Here I am my precious. Mama's here. I'm going to prepare our breakfast, but first I shall stand you next to the wall so that you can see me here. Princess Camille you're getting to be so tall! Soon I will have to buy you a new dress."

Lillianna busied herself looking into her sacks of food. She found some lettuce leaves, a few carrots and a really ripe banana which was soft and black on the outside. She washed the leaves and ate them; scraped the carrots with a knife and chewed them, finally eating the banana. She followed this with a drink of water and she was finished. Next she busied herself cleaning the interior of the large black pipe that Pedro had carried into her room many weeks earlier; he had laid it flat in the corner and covered it with stones. This would make a better home for Princess Camille and the linen curtain. This done she settled back on the bed with her doll and talked and played with it until she became drowsy and fell asleep.

The sound of a motor awakened Lillianna, and she sat up staring around the room trying to decide which day it was. She could tell by the beams of light on the wall that it was about lunch time. She looked down at Camille in her arms. It was still Sunday, but why then was there the sound of a motor? She quickly rose from the bed and took her crutch, leaving the princess Camille sleeping between the covers. The motor stopped and shortly thereafter she could hear the sound of voices nearby; one was that of a girl.

Lillianna went to the door, unbolted it and pushed it open. It fell to the ground making a loud noise. She emerged into the sunlight. There, on the side of the hill beside the heap of trash was a girl of about her age. She wore a white hat with a brim and her dark wavy hair hung down her back past her shoulders. She was so beautiful in her white dress embroidered with flowers and on her hands were little white laced gloves. Camille in all of her life had never seen anyone quite so beautiful. Beside her was a man in a gray uniform with a cap upon his head. He had white hair and was bent over with age. They turned toward Lillianna who stood leaning on her crutch by the entrance to the cave. The girl held one hand up to her face covering her nose. She climbed down the slope with the man slipping and struggling behind her, and she walked towards Lillianna.

"Please don't be afraid little girl." she had her hands spread out before her in a gesture of friendliness. "I would like to ask you a few questions." This little girl had an air of authority about her and Lillianna moved backwards a little, at the same time looking up at the man who had finally descended the slope.

"I would like to introduce myself. I am Maria Elaina Consuella Di Caprio, and this is our Chauffeur Enrico. Please don't be afraid." Lillianna straightened up and shuffled forward a few steps.

"I am not afraid." she uttered, surprised to find her voice. "What do you want?" The girl took a deep breath and wagged her head from side to side.

"Well it's a long story. I have a brother, a few years younger than myself, and we got into a beastly fight. Do you have a brother?"

"No, I don't." Maria looked at her chauffeur and shrugged her shoulders.

"You are lucky; they can be such an awful pain sometimes. Anyway we got into this fight, and to punish me he hid my little Paola from me. She is my doll you see, and we love each other very much." Tears came to her eyes as she continued. "Well, he hid her in one of our large lace curtains, which had been removed for cleaning. One of our new maids; whom I am happy to say, is no longer with us; thought that it was to be put in the trash. Imagine such beautiful lace made by many workers for hours and hours being put in the trash. The girl was a complete idiot!.Anyway she put it in the trash bin, which, I am told, eventually ends up here. So, I have come here to look for my Paola and am quite desperate to find her; she, of course will be so terribly frightened." She turned her face toward Lillianna. "Do you have a doll?" Lillianna hesitated.

"Yes I have one."

"Oh that's wonderful; then you will understand!"

Lillianna felt a terrible pain come over her, a pain that came with the realization that she must part with the most precious thing that had ever come into her life; something which had meant everything to her. A voice came from within her "I have your doll and your lace curtain. I know that if they were mine I would miss them so much too." Lillianna's chin began to quiver as she fought back tears, but she was still able to hold her head high. "Please stay there and I will get them for you."

Donna Elaina screamed with joy and running forward, threw her arms around Lillianna's neck. Lillianna stood immobile with her hands at her side, looking at Enrico who shuffled nervously holding his cap in both hands. "Please, this is not necessary." she said, and struggled with little success to break free of Donna Elaina's grasp. Finally Donna Elaina regained her composure and backed away from Lillianna who gasped,

"Now please wait here and I will get them for you."

Lillianna turned and limped towards the cave entrance, her head felt as though it would explode and she fought hard to hold back her tears. She walked to the bed, kneeled beside it, and folded up the lace until it was about the length of her bed. She then took Princess Camille and picked her up. 'Mama.' the doll said.

"No my Princess, I am not your mother, I am going to return you to your real mother who loves you and misses you very much." She took the doll in her arms and kissed her on both cheeks. "Now you be a good girl for your mother and make me proud of you!"

Donna Elaina, who was at the entrance to the cave, had witnessed everything, she crept silently away, her heart pounding wildly. Lillianna emerged from the cave with the bundle under her arm. "No harm has come to her. I have looked after her well." She handed the bundle to Enrico. Donna Elaina was ecstatic. She turned toward her chauffeur and said,

"Enrico, I must have her now, she must be so terribly frightened!"

Enrico nodded and said, "Yes Mademoiselle." He took the doll from the bundle and Donna Elaina swept it into her arms kissing her all over her face. She examined her all over, lifting up her dress and feeling her legs her long white socks and black shiny shoes. She held her upright and cried tears of joy as the doll opened its eyes and said 'Mama.'

Lillianna stood motionless; her face was without expression, like a mask. Her eyes were like two balls of fire staring into space. Enrico came towards Lillianna; his face though wrinkled with age was soft and tender.

"What is your name young lady?" He spoke slowly in a deep voice.

"I am Lillianna." she said moving backwards slightly on her crutch.

"Well Miss Lillianna, I am an old man, but this day you have made me very proud. I will not forget you. You will always be a princess to me.".He removed his cap, and then as a gesture of respect, bowed his head. He turned and walked away towards the hill. Donna Elaina followed him and turned to wave as she ran to his side. Together they climbed the hill, her hand in his.

Lillianna walked to the entrance of the cave. She picked up the door, and dragged it into the recess behind her. She bolted the door shut and walked to her bed. Tossing her crutch aside, she dove onto the rags and collapsed, sobbing loudly upon her pillow.

Enrico opened the rear door of the limousine and waited for Donna Elaina to enter. He handed her the doll and took the material with him to the front seat.

"Enrico put the air conditioning on! I'm baking in here!" The words flowed freely from her mouth and she spoke without looking up, as she was busy with her doll, adjusting her dress and placing her on the plush leather seat beside her.

"Right away Miss Donna." called Enrico through the intercom.

"Now my precious little Paola you must tell me all about your adventures. You were so brave living among the rats and mice and that terrible, terrible smell. When Mama gets you home, she's going to put you into a big bath of hot rose scented water and wash you all over. Then

I'm going to feed you. My poor baby you must be starving!"

Enrico drove slowly along the track towards the city. There were pot holes and dips in the surface but the limo glided effortlessly over them along the path. Soon they reached the highway and passed by hundreds of little shacks on the edge of the city. As they climbed the hill towards the city center, shacks gave way to high rise buildings and clean paved streets. Large department stores displayed mannequins with the latest fashions in clothing. There were restaurants with beautiful entranceways and doormen ready to receive patrons and to park their cars. Large luxury cars were everywhere, with well dressed chauffeurs standing by them in the mid day sun. Their patrons, usually women, ambled through the stores picking out dresses for their cocktail parties.

Enrico took a turning to the right, and soon they were on a wide boulevard with mansions so large they would better be described as Chateaus. He turned into the entrance of one of these mansions and stopped in front of the large steel gates. A wall about three meters high surrounded the property on both sides as far as the eye could see. A man appeared from a sentry box beside the gates. He was old and was dressed like Enrico, and he walked with a limp. He pressed a button and the gates slowly opened. He waved to Enrico as the limousine glided by and started along the long winding boulevard lined with trees and flowering shrubs to the main house. Gardeners bent at their work maintaining the grounds hardly looked up as the limousine passed by.........

A maid was standing at the foot of the stairs on the

gravel driveway in front of the main entrance as the limousine came to a stop in front of her. The maid rushed forward and opened the rear door of the Limousine to allow Donna Elaina to exit. She smiled as she saw the excitement on Dona Elaina's face.

"You found her Miss Donna! You found her! I can hardly believe it!"

"Yes Therese, I found her in the most abominable of conditions. She was living in the utmost squalor, next to a huge rubbish heap. Fortunately a little urchin had taken her in and put her in a cave where she passed the night. She must have been terribly frightened."

"All's well that ends well, Miss Donna. Come in out of this heat." said the maid as she reached forward to take her hand. Donna Elaina got out of the car and climbed the stairs to the entrance of the mansion. She turned back to Enrico who was standing beside the car his hat in his hand.

"Enrico." she called out. "Give that curtain to Therese; and you Therese; put it with the others and take them to be cleaned right away."

"Right away Miss Donna." said the maid, bowing her head as she did so.

Donna Elaina climbed the marble stairway with her doll under her arm. As she approached her room along the corridor a maid appeared.

"Who are you?" demanded Donna Elaina looking the maid over from head to toe. The maid curtsied.

"I am Angelina Miss Donna; the new maid".

"Well Angelina, pour me a bath right away and lay out a new set of clothing for me, I have just returned from

Hell; and Angelina, bring some sandwiches and some peach juice and put them on my table by the window. I don't wish to be disturbed for the rest of the day.

"Yes Miss Donna." the maid bowed her head and opened the door to Donna Elaina's room. She walked quickly by the large four posted bed, and disappeared into the bathroom. Donna Elaina put her doll up to her shoulder and patted her gently on the back as she walked over to the bed and laid her upon a pillow. She bent down and whispered in her doll's ear.

"That's right my baby, close your eyes and sleep for a while, you must be so exhausted; but you're home now! Mama will be just next door taking a bath."

Donna Elaina went into the bathroom discarding her clothes as she walked. She stepped into the bath, and sank below the foam. She floated with her nose just above the foam and rubbed her face clean with a warm soapy sponge. She shuddered, as she tried to rid herself of the terrible smell that seemed to stay within her nostrils, she could not forget the images that flashed through her mind of what she had seen that day. She thought of the little girl who had found her baby Paola. Of her eyes; large black eyes filled with pain, set in a thin brown face, a girl hobbling around on a crutch. She scrubbed her body with a foam pad, stood up and rinsed herself off in the shower.

She emerged from the bathroom in a large white bath robe with a towel wrapped around her head. Angelina had picked up her clothes and had left the room. She ran over and sat at the table, and started to eat her sandwiches. She drank her peach juice, looking occasionally at her doll Paola who was lying upon a pillow with her eyes closed.

She wiped her face with the back of her hand and walked over to the bed and slipped beneath its covers pulling her doll close to her side. Once again she smelled the foul odors of the dump as she rested her head next to her doll.

"Paola my darling, you don't smell so good. Mama's going to give you a bath; but not now; tomorrow." she said, turning her back on her baby. The emotions she had felt and sights that she had seen that day had left her exhausted. She had not been able to sleep the night before, and although it was just after lunch she felt very tired. She yawned several times. She turned once more to a Paola. "Yes, Mama will take care of you later, but she's very tired now. Welcome home my baby, mother loves you." The words trailed off. They were her last, as she was soon in the land of dreams.

Chapter 3

It was nearly 10 am when Donna Elaina stirred in her bed. She stretched her arms out and yawned. Sun was streaming through the windows announcing another oppressively hot day. Fortunately, the heat remained on the outside. She could hear the swishing of cool air as it came from the ducts above her head on the far side of the room. The events of yesterday had shocked her, and she realized that she had been in bed for almost twenty hours. Quite suddenly she sat upright in bed and turned towards her doll. She let out a cry of happiness.

"Paola my baby, it's so good to have you back here beside me". She reached over and pulled the doll towards her.

"Mama" the doll cried, as Donna Elaina lifted her up.

"What is it my precious?" she said. And then she caught her breath as she looked into her dolls eyes. "Why my baby, you've been crying." Paola's eyes were moist with tears. "It's not possible!" yelled Donna Elaina. "I've never seen you cry before! What is it my baby? Tell Mama!" A tear left her dolls eye and trickled down her cheek. "Tell me what is it? Are you hurt, or something?"

She began to feel her doll all over. "I know what it is." she said sniffing at her clothes. "It's your dress it smells so terribly bad. Let me take it off. Mama will have it cleaned right away." She started to unbutton the dress in the front until it was open down to her dolls waist. She pulled it off her shoulders and it fell to the bed where her doll was standing. Donna Elaina let out a gasp of surprise. "What has happened to you my baby? What has happened to your leg?" It was hardly believable, but one of Paola's legs was about a centimeter shorter than the other. Even the doll's foot and ankle appeared to be smaller on this leg; without the cross strap on her shoe, it surely would have fallen off. Donna Elaina put her hand over her mouth and blew breath through her fingers, a habit she had formed at an early age whenever things made her nervous or she came face to face with something she could not explain. She pressed on the buzzer next to her bed, and sat leaning against the head board clutching her doll next to her chest.

A knock sounded at the door to her room and a maid entered and walked quickly to her bedside.

"Good morning Miss Donna, what would you like me to do for you?"

"I would like to see my parents! Are they in?"

"No Miss. We expect them back tomorrow afternoon at about noon." Donna Elaina frowned looking down at her hands before speaking.

"Prepare my usual breakfast. I will eat it in my room."

"Right away, Miss Donna." The maid bowed her head, before walking backwards out of the room.

"Come now my baby Mama's going to take care of you." She picked the doll up and hugged her close to her body. The doll said Mama. Donna Elaina walked to the bathroom and laid her doll on the wash stand, where she removed her clothes, stockings and shoes. There was a knock at the door and the maid entered with a tray of breakfast cereals and fruit. Donna Elaina collected all of her Paola's clothing together, including the dolls dress which was on the bed and gave them to the maid.

"Here. Take these and have them cleaned immediately."

"Yes Miss Donna," The maid, bowed her head again before walking swiftly towards the door. Donna Elaina returned to her doll and started to wash it with a moist flannel over its entire body, taking care to gently rub around the affected areas of its left leg and foot. She then took a paper tissue and cleaned the dolls black shoes until they shone brightly. "Come with me my baby." she said. "You must be so hungry. Let's go and have the nice breakfast Jessica has prepared for us."

When Donna Elaina descended the large marble stairs into the Grand Entrée, she was met by her big brother Victor Emanuel. He was tall, lean, had curly dark brown hair, brown eyes and was extremely handsome; he had just returned from riding, and carried a riding crop which he held in his hands behind his back.

"Well Donna. I see that you are reunited with your

Paola, and she looks none the worse for her adventure." He walked towards her and kissed her lightly on her cheek. It was true Paola was dressed in her lace dress. Her hair was combed and shone in the light reflected down from the clearstory windows.

"Nothing could be farther from the truth dear brother. She arrived here yesterday in the most horrid state. We found her in the dump, exactly where you had suggested that we go to look for her!"

Her brother motioned her towards the marble stairs where he took a seat and held out his hand and helped her sit down beside him.

"So what then is so horrible?" he asked. Donna pulled up her dolls dress and pointed to its legs.

"This!" She exclaimed. Victor Emanuel looked hard at the doll, frowned a little and said.

"This what?"

"Her leg! Just look at it! Don't you see that it is smaller than the other one?" Donna pointed to the each leg. Victor Emanuelle wagged his head from side to side, his brown curls falling down across his forehead.

"That! That's it!" he laughed. "Well it is a little smaller, but hardly noticeable, especially under that dress. She may have been crushed in the rubble yesterday. It's nothing to worry about little one."

"Victor!" she screamed, exasperated at such little show of emotion he had displayed toward her Paola. "Do you know that this morning when I awoke, she had tears in her eyes, real tears that ran down her face?" Victor Emanuelle looked toward the ceiling directly above him. His eyes ran along the banisters on the second floor. He breathed out a long sigh.

"Well my little princess, why don't you put her in bed so that she can get plenty of rest and we will see how she is tomorrow." Donna Elaina thought for a few seconds.

"Thank you Victor; you always know what to do."

"Well that's good: Hurry and put her into bed, we both have tutors coming to give us lessons, and I must hurry to prepare for a tough geography exam. I'll wait for you in the library." They both walked upstairs to their rooms.

Five minutes later Victor Emanuel descended the stairs at high speed with several books in his hand and walked along the corridor to the library. A door slammed upstairs and Donna Elaina hurried along the corridor. She took the stairs one at a time, her books in one hand and the hand-rail in the other; she too hurried along the corridor to the library

That evening Victor Emanuel and Donna Elaina were joined at the dining table by their little brother Umberto. He was fighting with his nanny as he entered the room and his nanny appeared to be quite distressed Victor Emanuel stood and wiped his mouth with his serviette.

"Thank you Maria." he said. Followed by; "Umberto, you are late for grace. This is the second time this week. Please sit down now!" A maid pulled out Umberto's seat and he sat upon it. He was a handsome little boy with a head full of black curly hair. His nose was covered with freckles and his eyes were dark green; quite unlike Victor Emanuel who's eyes were as black as coal. They bowed their heads as Victor Emanuel blessed the meal.

Two maids who had their backs resting against the

wall with their heads bowed came forward with dishes of food which had been resting on the sideboard near the door. The three were served a meal of roast duck, with rice and vegetables. They ate in silence, Donna Elaina glancing several times at Umberto who kept his head down averting her gaze. The silence was broken by Victor Emanuel, who wiped his mouth with his serviette.

"Umberto, there is a serious problem that I wish to address to you. That which concerns Donna's doll Paola." Umberto's eyes grew wide with fear as he stared at Victor Emanuel

"It was an accident Victor. Donna was teasing me in front of her friend Sarah, telling me that I was a stupid little boy who knew nothing. I was embarrassed and thought that I would teach her a lesson. I hid her doll inside some drapes that were leaning against a wall in the library."

Victor Emanuel paused for a few moments, resting his elbows on the table and tapping one hand on the back of the other. "Well young man, your foolishness had very serious consequences. A maid; who is no longer with us, picked up that bundle, and put it out for the trash. Donna's doll and that beautiful lace drape ended up in the city refuse pile." Umberto let out a gasp.

"Surely the drape was taken down for cleaning. I don't understand why it would have gone to the city pile." Umberto was shaken and close to tears.

"That is why the maid is no longer with us." repeated Victor Emanuel. "Now, I know that you were not completely guilty for the chain of events that led to the doll going to the dump, but you certainly started them, and it brought a great deal of stress upon your sister, who, very fortunately, had the idea of going to the dump to look for her doll. But for an act of god and the sheer honesty of a little girl at the dump, all may not have ended quite so well."

"Are you saying that you got the doll and drapes back?" said Umberto, his eyes wide with disbelief.

"Yes, although I am not sure of their condition. I shall have to discipline you for all the trouble you have caused, unless you prefer that I speak to Father?"

"No Victor! Please don't speak to Father!" Victor Emanuel leaned back against the tall leather head rest on his chair.

"Very well then, I shall need time to decide on what it is that I want you to do. Tomorrow, by the way, Father and Mother will arrive at about 12 A.M. We must all be up, dressed, and ready to greet them. Is that understood?" The two children said yes and the subject was closed.

Later that night, Donna Elaina returned to her bedroom .and picked her doll up. The doll said 'Mama' as always. She looked pretty in her clean dress, with her flaxen hair combed and shiny. Donna Elaina lifted up her dress. The left leg was the same as earlier that day. She thought that perhaps in time she would get used to it and decided that it was a small price to pay for having her baby returned to her. She laid her doll on the pillow, covered her with bed-covers and went to the bathroom to clean her teeth. She returned a few minutes later and slipped into bed beside her doll, putting her arm around her. A few minutes later she was sound asleep.

Chapter 4

IT MUST HAVE BEEN about 8.30.am, when a terrible scream came from the bedroom of Donna Elaina. A maid who was walking along the corridor, rushed to her room. Downstairs in the kitchen a bell rang and the maids looked up at the Annunciation Board. Room No. 5

"That's Miss Donna Elaina's room," said the senior kitchen chef. "Go and see what she wants Jose." Jose left the room and ran along the corridor to the Grand Entrée. From the foot of the stairs she could hear Donna Elaina sobbing loudly. She ran up the stairs as quickly as she could and entered Donna Elaina's bedroom. Maria the other maid was at the side of the bed holding Donna Elaina in her arms.

"What is it?" she said "What is wrong Maria?" Maria took the doll from Donna Elaina. Tears were falling slowly from the dolls eyes. Jose made the sign of the cross in front of her and took the doll and laid it down on the bed.

"Take a look at her legs!" sobbed Donna Elaina. "Just look at them!" The maid lifted the dolls dress. The dolls left leg was missing completely below the knee. "I've looked in the bed and there is no stocking or shoe to be found!" said Donna Elaina as she broke into heavy sobbing. "I don't understand! I don't understand!" she moaned in a low voice. Both maids crossed themselves, and knelt at the side of the bed and started to pray. Maria spoke in a voice crazed with fear.

"Jose, go and summon Victor Emanuel. This is too much for me to handle."

Jose ran from the room and along the corridor stopping outside Victor Emanuel's bedroom. She stood for a moment frozen with fear. Then finding courage within her, knocked on his door and entered the room. Victor Emanuel sat up in bed.

"What is it woman? Have you seen a ghost or something?"

"It's Miss Donna Elaina sir!"

"My god is she ill?" said Victor Emanuel jumping from his bed and pulling a silk dressing gown around him.

"No sir. It's her doll. Something terrible has happened to it!"

Victor Emanuel ran his hand through his hair. Somewhat relieved, he regained his composure. "Something has happened to her doll Paola, you say?"

"Yes Sir!"

"Very well, tell her that I'll be right there."

"Yes sir." said the maid as she scurried from the room

Victor Emanuel went to the bathroom and combed his hair. He stepped into his slippers, at the same time tying a knot in the belt around his waist. He left the room and walked along the corridor at a quick pace to his sister's room. Donna Elaina lay weeping on her pillow. She raised herself up as Victor Emanuel entered the room. "Victor!" She cried. "Look at her leg today. Just look at it!" Victor Emanuel went to the doll which was laying face up on the bed. He could see that the doll had been crying or at least had manufactured some false tears. He lifted the dolls dress as the maids, standing far back from the bed, made the sign of the cross.

What he saw next amazed even him. The doll's left leg was missing to just above the knee. There was no sign of a rip or a seam. Just a smooth end as though it had always been there. The shoe and stocking were missing, and nowhere to be found. He turned to his sister who held her hands in her ashen face, her thumbs pressing into her chin. Her eyes were swollen from crying.

"My dear sister, please do not cry, there has to be a logical explanation for this. Your doll, after all, is not human."

"You are wrong Victor." she said. "Paola is human, I know she is! She has become like that little urchin at the dump."

"What are you talking about?" he said, a furrow appearing upon his brow. "What little urchin at the dump?"

"The little girl at the dump, who gave Paola back to me, was walking with a crutch. She had her left leg missing above the knee! Don't you see? The little girl saved Paola from the trash and took her into a cave where she lived at the foot of the pile."

Victor Emanuel nodded his head from side to side. He

had been sitting on the bed, but stood up and started to pace backwards and forwards in the room, his hand rubbing his chin. "This is too much for me." he said. "I shall talk to father about it when he comes. Until such time we should say nothing to anyone. Instead we should all prepare for his arrival." The maids left the room and ran down the corridor, anxious to be away from the whole mysterious affair.

Shortly before lunch, a large black limousine could be seen coming along the tree lined route to the house. The entire household staff was standing at the foot of the stairs. Victor Emanuel stood at the head of the stairs with his young sister and brother. As the limo pulled up in front of the entrance, Enrico, who was standing at the head of the line, removed his hat and walked forward to open the rear door of the car. Señor Carlos Emanuel Di Caprio stepped out, and reached in to take the hand of his wife Isabella. They were dressed in city clothes, he in a dark blue silk suit, and she in a formal red dress. She was exceptionally beautiful tall and slim, a head taller than her husband, and perhaps fifteen years younger. Señor Carlos was balding slightly and showed signs of a man who liked his food and drink, in that he had a rather large belly.

The children descended the stairs, Victor Emanuel first. He shook hands with his father and kissed his mother on the cheek, he was followed by his siblings. Some men walked forward to remove the luggage from the limousine, and the family went into the house. A maid arrived and took their street clothes. Isabella took Umberto by the hand and they all walked into the library. Going to the library was a ritual that always took place when the parents returned from a long trip.

"Well children", said Señor Carlos "what do you have to report?" Donna Elaina burst into tears and ran towards her father, who was seated in an upright chair besides the fireplace, and she buried her face in his lap. "Good heavens child!" he said. "What could be so bad? Tell your father all about it."

"Well father, it would probably be better if I explained." said Victor Emanuel.

"Please do so!" said Señor Di Caprio, gently rubbing Donna Elaina's head with his hand.

"It's about Donna's doll Paola." Isabella who had rushed to comfort her child appeared somewhat relieved when she heard the news.

"What is wrong with Paola my child?" she said. Victor Emanuel continued.

"Somehow the doll became entwined in the drapes from the dining room that you had ordered to be cleaned. By the most unfortunate twist of fate, a drape, with the doll inside of it, ended up in our trash bins. They in turn were taken by the dumpster to the land fill on the outskirts of the city." Isabella put her hand to her mouth and let out a gasp. "Don't worry mother everything is now under control; that is almost everything. First thing I did was to get rid of the maid who really wasn't on our staff, but had come in to help her sister. Donna Elaina, realizing what had happened to her doll, asked Enrico to take her to the land fill. Thanks to her quick action she was able to retrieve all the objects including her doll."

The father who had been listening, and who was running his hand through his daughter's hair, raised his hand. "What I would like to know is how the doll came to be in the middle of the drapes." Umberto, who was sitting very quietly on his seat looking down at his hands, spoke.

"It was I father. I hid the doll from Donna because she embarrassed me in front of her friend Sarah." Señor Carlos looked at his youngest son, and then at his daughter.

"I shall return to this later" he said, making a gesture with his hand for Victor Emanuel to continue. His eyes rested once more on his youngest son. He paused for a moment, then, with a flurry waived his finger at his eldest son. "Continue!" he said.

"Well Father, the drape is finally being cleaned along with the others. It was when Donna Elaina was removing the dress of her doll that she noticed that the left leg had shrunk."

"Shrunk!" said both parents in chorus.

"Donna told me that she remembers having examined her doll fully while she was still at the land fill, and saw nothing wrong. It was only on the following morning when she noticed tears in the dolls eyes that she decided to change her dress, thinking that she was in such a state because her dress was smelling so badly. That is when she saw the dolls left leg was a little shorter but that it still retained its stocking and shoe. She asked me to look at it, which I did.

Señor Carlos shrugged his shoulders. "If the doll went to the dump in a dumpster, I am not at all surprised that it was a little crushed. It would have been a miracle had it been otherwise!"

"I came to the same conclusion Sir." said Victor Emanuel, his brow furrowing as he glanced quickly towards his mother who was passing the rosary through her hands. "However the following morning, I was again summoned to her room early by one of the maids, and there I saw not only that the doll appeared to have been crying again, but that this time the dolls leg was far worse. It was now devoid of both the stocking and shoe, and the leg was now missing to right above the left knee. We searched in the bed for the shoe and stocking but they were nowhere to be found."

Isabella became pale and made the sign of the cross across in front of her heart. The father placed a finger on his lip, motioning his wife to stay calm.

"And how do you account for this my son?" he said.

"Well sir. I think Donna Elaina could best explain that. Donna do you think you could do that?" Donna Elaina turned to face the family, sitting on her fathers lap her hands firmly planted on his knees. She looked at her mother.

"Momma, Enrico and I went to the land fill early Sunday morning. We had begun to search among that foul smelling refuse, when we saw a wretched little girl about my age looking at us from the bottom of the pile. I shall never forget my feet sinking into that awful mess!" She paused, closed her eyes and lifted her head in disgust before continuing. "We approached the little girl and I asked her if she had seen the doll and the drape; she said that she had, and that they were safe in her home. I followed her into this black hole in the rocks, which served, I presume as her home. I saw her in there kissing Paola and rolling her up in the curtain drape. I ducked back outside and waited for her to bring them to me; which she did."

"How very kind of her to do that!" exclaimed the mother. "It must have been very difficult for her to have returned the doll to you. She had probably never seen anything quite as pretty in her life."

Victor Emanuel stood up and walked over to the back of the chair where his mother was sitting. He put both hands upon her shoulders and looking down into her eyes, he spoke almost in a whisper, as if he didn't want the others to hear "Mother, this is the thing which is so strange and a little frightening. The little girl had only one leg! The mother grasped her heart and looked up at Victor Emanuel. Her eyes were wide open and her mouth sagged at the corners. He continued, kneeling beside her, cradling her in his arms. "She was standing there with a crutch and her left leg was missing just above the knee, exactly the same as Donna Elaina's doll." Isabella crossed herself again. This time her face had became quite pale, she looked at her husband.

"Did you hear what Victor is saying Carlos? What can all this mean?"

"Calm yourself my dear" said Señor Carlos, removing Donna Elaina from his knee and standing up. "There must be a logical explanation for all of this. What we do know is that dolls aren't human." His voice trailed off. "But just the same they can be used, perhaps, to convey a message, an intermediary of sorts; a messenger, to bring our attention to something. Donna Elaina, go and bring the doll to me! I want to look at it for myself." Donna Elaina put her arms on her waist and looked up at her father.

"Father! Paola is a her, not an it!" she said in dismay as she left the room in tears followed by Victor Emanuel. Umberto, seeing that he was alone with his parents and feeling their eyes upon him, left his chair and ran from the room.

Señor Carlos stood up, and with his hands clasped behind his back and started to pace the floor. Isabella closed her eyes, made the sign of the cross and bowed her head in prayer. A few moments later Victor Emanuel returned with the doll under one arm, followed by Donna Elaina and Umberto, who remained at the door. "There you are father" he said lifting up the dolls dress. "You will note that the leg while missing just above the knee shows no sign of having been ripped off, on the contrary it looks as if it had always been that way; no stitches or anything. Also when I lifted her from the bed she did have what appeared to be tears in her eyes, as she had on a previous occasion."

Señor Carlos took Victor Emanuel by the arm and looked into his eyes. "Victor," he said, "I know you to be an honest young man, and I am very proud of the way you comport yourself, and so I ask you in all seriousness, was this doll in the same condition the first time that you saw her?"

"No sir, she was absolutely not like that! Her leg was longer; almost the same length as the other, and she had a foot, albeit a little smaller than the other foot, but a foot; this I swear."

"Very well then; it is settled; we will go Sunday morning to visit this young girl to see what is to be done." Victor Emanuel went to his mother and put his arm around her.

"Don't worry mother. Father and I will get to the bottom of this and all will be well. I promise!"

The parents rose and left the room, Umberto taking care to move out of their way. When they had passed by he came back into the room and spoke to Victor Emanuel. "Victor. I am truly sorry for what I have done and wish to know what it is that I must do to make amends." Victor ran his hand through his young brother's hair.

"Umberto," he said "I believe that which has happened, happened for a reason, and you were merely a pawn in these events. This goes far beyond the actions of one person, and we must follow our lead to see where it takes us. I don't want you to dwell upon this nor feel guilty, for I believe now, that it was beyond your control. I would like you to comfort your sister in all of this and to persuade her that all will be well in the end. Will you do that for me?" Umberto looked up at his brother with admiration in his eyes.

"Not only will I try to comfort her, but I will strive to be more like you." Victor Emanuel smiled, bent down and kissed his brother on his brow. Although he was smiling, he could see his brother's eyes, large and dark beginning to haze over as tears welled up around the edges.

"Be off with you little brother!" he said as he tapped him on the rear end. Umberto ran off laughing through his tears. Victor Emanuel crossed himself and left the room.

Chapter 5

SUNDAY MORNING ARRIVED. MAIDS were busy closing windows as the sun rose higher in the sky. They had been up for a few hours and had opened them, to allow in the cooler night air through the screens, but now it was time to close them against the oppressive heat of the day. Soon the monsoon season would be upon them and the air would take on the odor of damp leaves and moist earth. Birds would sing in the trees and monkeys would frolic in the pools and in the hollows. It was not a good time for snakes as the monsoon ditches, filled to capacity, would send torrents of water by, entrapping and drowning many in their path. That season had not yet arrived however, and this morning Señor Carlos DiCapprio and his son Victor Emanuel would seek solace in the air conditioned comfort of the Limousine.

Enrico, stooped a little from the onset of old age, removed his hat as he opened the rear door of the car. He had a shock of thick black hair with white strands running through it especially on the sides, his bushy eyebrows and a handle bar moustache were of the same color. His eyes drooped. They were kindly eyes, humble eyes and they twinkled. He was an honest man who sought nothing more than to serve others the best way he could, and this he had done for three generations of the DiCaprio family. At the last moment Donna Elaina arrived with her baby Paola in her arms. "What are you doing here at this hour?" said Victor Emanuel. His father smiled.

"Well since you are here." he said, "You may as well come along. You could be useful."

The four of them drove out of the suburbs and down the hill into town. They were soon in the poorer section on the outskirts of the city, and finally into the countryside, with its little hamlets dotting the roadside. The buzzer sounded and Enrico pressed a button, and a paneled window glided open behind him. "Yes sir." he said, at the same time looking into the rear view mirror.

"Enrico is there any way to the landfill other than the one you took with my daughter?" said Señor Carlos looking at Enrico's eyes in the mirror.

"Yes sir, I am going to drive into the little village at the foot of the landfill. There is a roadway there where trucks pick up workers from the village to go into town. It is not paved, but is in fairly good condition."

"Thank you Enrico. That will be all."

"Yes sir." Enrico pressed the button and the glass panel to the rear of him slid closed. Señor Carlos turned to his son.

"I was wondering how we were in fact going to climb

down to the bottom of the landfill through all that mess, if the girl is living where you say she is."

Donna Elaina was talking to her doll telling her not to be afraid, and that they were just going to see the nice lady who rescued her from the heap, and then they would return home.

"Sir," said Victor Emanuel. "How does Enrico know where all these little roads are, so far from our home?" Señior Carlos thought for a moment and then turning to Victor said,

"Well my son. I believe he may have come from a squatter area himself, perhaps even this one, or one nearby, though it would have certainly been more than fifty years ago. I doubt that he would know anyone there now. He seldom talks about his past, but the story my father told me is that when he was a young man he fell in love with a girl from his village. She married another, and at that time he left and took up employment with your grandfather. He never married, and has remained loyal to our family ever since."

"How terribly sad that is father!"

"Perhaps, but at that time the job of a chauffeur was to be on call twenty-four hours a day, not so much different from that which it is today. He ironed his Master's suits and prepared him for the days activities. There was no real free time for him. In this respect we now have a maid to do that and so he does have more free time. In return for all this, he ate downstairs with the staff, was paid a wage and had accommodation above the garage. Much as it is today in fact. Today however his conditions are far better than he had then. Why he has a kitchen and a radio etc."

The road they were taking sloped down and narrowed to scarcely more than a track. Vegetation became thicker and bamboo loomed up each side of the limousine, linking in the canopy above. The blinding rays and oppressive heat of the sun were locked outside and the area would have become a thick impenetrable jungle were it not for people from the village constantly cutting and pruning the undergrowth to keep this artery to the outside world open. They turned a bend in the road and quite suddenly they were on the outskirts of a village. There was a motley collection of lean-to's, some with a patchwork of corrugated roofs of different sizes, but for the most part neat bamboo roofs. As they arrived at the center of the village, they saw women waiting in line to fill their buckets from a faucet at the side of the road. Little children stood naked while mothers or older siblings washed and poured water over them. The faucet was attached to a vertical pipe which came out of the ground. As the limousine crept silently by the faucet,.children, barefoot and dressed in little more than rags stopped their playing and moved to the side of the road and peered into the limousine, their eyes seemingly too large for their little faces.

Enrico drove through the village to the other end and stopped next to a stream in front of the last house. He pressed the button to open the sliding panel. "Sir," he said. "With your permission, I will ask for directions at this house. I believe the landfill is on the other side of that little opening ahead, but I fear that it will be too narrow for the limousine."

"Go ahead Enrico, we shall wait here." said Señor Di Caprio, peering up at the house on the slope at his left. Enrico slowly mounted the wooden steps to the house, leaning heavily on the guard rail for support. The house was in better condition than most and appeared to have more than one room, as it was fairly long. He was met at the top of the stairs by a man in his early forties. He was lean and handsome and had a head of thick black curly hair. They spoke for a while and Enrico motioned towards the Limousine. Other people joined him on the porch. Some girls and a young man, finally an older woman appeared with a little girl who was holding her hand.

Suddenly Donna Elaina screamed, "That's her, that's the little girl with one leg!" She started to wave to the girl who was shaking hands with Enrico.

"Why don't you open the door and get out." Victor Emanuel said to his little sister. "She surely can't see you there behind this smoked glass." Donna Elaina tucked her doll under her arm and took her father's hand. The three of them stepped out of the car.

The heat of the sun was oppressive and they walked over to the shade of a tree. Enrico descended the stairs and slowly made his way to Señor Carlos. He was overheating in his chauffeur's suit, which was buttoned up to the neck, and with his large peaked hat pulled down tightly on his head, there was very little area for his skin to breathe. "Sir," he said pausing for a breath. "They wish to know if you would like to enter their home where you could discuss what it is that you want from them."

Senior Di Caprio looked into Enrico's eyes. Enrico was breathing heavily and appeared quite pale. "I will go and see them Enrico, but first I want you to get in the car, keep the engine running and put the air conditioning on maximum to cool yourself off. I will take care of this."

"Yes sir. Thank you sir." he said breathing heavily, his eyes barely open. Victor Emanuel took his arm and helped him around the side of the car to the driver's seat. "Bless you sir." he said.

People from the village began to gather some distance from the car. It was not every day that something akin to this occurred in their village. The Di- Caprio family climbed the stairs together. Victor Emanuel had taken the doll in one hand and held his sister's hand with the other. He was very tall, lean and strikingly handsome and he had about him a certain regal appearance. He wore a light sports coat and a tie. His father was wearing a bow tie with a starched collar and formal black suit. It was the same type of attire that he always wore. Some of the household staff speculated that he even slept in it. Almost before she reached the top step Donna Elaina demanded to have her Paola. She walked over to the girl with the crutch and said. "Good morning little girl do you remember me?"

"Yes. I remember you," said Lillianna, a slight smile lighting up her face. "You are Miss Donna Elaina."

"And you? I don't remember your name."

"It is Lillianna."

"Ah yes!" said Donna Elaina." "I am so happy to meet you again Lillianna. This of course is Paola whom you so kindly rescued from certain death. I shall be eternally grateful to you for that."

"Thank you Miss Donna Elaina." Said Lillianna completely charmed and mystified by the words that flowed from Donna Elaina's lips; words that were unlike any she had heard before. Although they were about the same age, they were worlds apart. It was probably at that moment that the desire to learn to read and write took over her whole being.

Señor Carlos followed Alfredo into the house; he looked neither right nor left, but simply went to the seats that were proffered to him and to his son. Alfredo and Maria sat opposite. He clasped his hands together on the table. They were soft well manicured hands with a series of large diamond encrusted rings on several fingers. He looked into the eyes of Alfredo and spoke. "I would like to explain the reason why I have been drawn here to your home, and I would also like to put to rest some very strange and inexplicable circumstances regarding the bizarre events that have happened in my house since the return of my daughter's doll."

Alfredo and Maria looked at each other quizzically. They appeared to be completely mystified by what was taking place. At that moment Vivienne came to the table. She was dressed simply but had about her a refined look, and a beauty that simply startled Victor Emanuel. She introduced herself to both Señor Carlos and Victor Emanuel. Both men stood up. Victor Emanuel for a moment lost his composure. Vivienne smiled politely at the men and took a seat next to her mother. The two men sat down and Victor Emanuel spoke.

"I think, that is, it would be better," he said, "if we started at the beginning. You may not be aware of any of the circumstances leading up to this meeting. You see my little sister Donna Elaina, lost her doll, and by a series of unfortunate events, this doll ended up in the city land fill, where young Lillianna; I believe that is the name of your daughter; found it. When my sister, in her distress, came to the landfill next day with our chauffeur, to look for her doll, she met Lillianna, who seeing her distress, returned my sister's doll to her." Alfredo waved his hand in front of him.

"Well sir, this is a mystery to us. You see Lillianna is not our daughter, though we treat her like one of ours. She lives alone near the land fill. She told us nothing about finding a doll."

Señor Carlos tugged on his collar with his thumb and index finger. He was feeling the heat and humidity, much more than that in town. "We are sorry about the confusion." he said. "What I am about to tell you is so very strange that I can scarcely believe it myself." "When my daughter retrieved the doll from your, err…, Lillianna, she was careful to look at it all over to ensure that nothing was broken. This included looking at its arms and legs. The next day she was alarmed to find that her dolls left leg was a little shorter than the right, and that it had been crying real tears. I was not there at the time and so I didn't see all this. However my son was there and he confirmed that the doll's left leg was a little shorter. He assumed that the dolls left leg had been crushed in transit, which I think is reasonable to assume given the enormous loads those trucks, carry, and he did not feel too concerned about its condition.

Alfredo and Maria crossed themselves and Maria rose and took her rosary from the sideboard. She returned to the table and started passing the beads through her hands, below the table. Señor Carlos continued. "The next morning its condition was worse. I was not there at the time but my son will gladly reconfirm."

Victor Emanuel leaned forward slightly in his chair, his brow creased as he relived the moment "Yes I can tell you that the doll had tears in its eyes on both occasions and its left leg has shrunk until it resembled that of little Lillianna. You may examine it for yourselves. There are absolutely no tears on the leg in question. It is as if it were manufactured that way." The women and Alfredo crossed themselves.

Lillianna entered the room with Donna Elaina, who was holding her doll in her arms. "Bring the doll to me my little one." said Señor Carlos. Donna Elaina put her doll on the table and lifted up its dress. Once again the women crossed themselves.

"What does this mean?" said Alfredo, who suddenly appeared quite startled.

"We don't know." said Señor Carlos. "What I am about to propose to you now is that with your permission we would take Lillianna with us today, and tomorrow have her fitted with a prosthesis, which would serve her until she is an adult. At that time we will have a permanent one fitted."

Seeing that there seemed to be some confusion on the faces of the family across from him Victor Emanuel spoke up "My father speaks of his desire to have, with your permission, Lillianna fitted with an artificial leg, so that she could walk without a crutch. This leg would be adjusted until she has grown to full height. When that time arrives, she should be fitted with a permanent leg, which in color and shape would be quite difficult to distinguish from a real one."

Lillianna let out a gasp and put her hand to her mouth. She could not believe what she was hearing, nor could she understand why.

Maria who had been silent until now spoke out. "Sir, what you would like to do for Lillianna is most noble, but there are sadly, many people like her in this camp, some who are blind, others who have terrible diseases."

Señor Carlos cut her short. "Madam; we are most grateful to Lillianna for returning the doll to Donna Elaina. Such honesty and selflessness must not go unrewarded.".

"There is also another reason, if we are to be completely honest with you." said Victor Emanuel "That is, I am not able to explain why an inanimate doll, should progressively loose its leg, especially when it is the identical leg of the one who saved her from a terrible fate."

"It was a terrible fate Sir, as you say." said Alfredo. "But this is a doll, and in my time here I have seen far worse on that heap. Of course we would not stand in the way of Lillianna having a new leg, she promised that she would come and live with us, if ever she got a new one. What I would like to know Sir is when would you take her, and for how long?"

Señor Carlos who always made quick decisions about everything said. "I would like to take her with us now. My driver will return with her tomorrow or the day after, at the latest, if it is agreeable to you. At this time it would only be a temporary leg which would serve her until she is fully grown. It is later that she may have something more substantial which I will.be happy to pay for."

Alfredo took Lillianna in his arms. Would you like to go now with these gentlemen?".Lillianna cupped her hand over his ear and whispered into it. Alfredo turned and looked at Señor Di Caprio. "Sir, she tells me that she would like to go but would be too scared to go with you."

"That is very understandable. After all she doesn't know us." said Victor Emanuel, looking across at Vivienne. "Maybe we could persuade mademoiselle Vivienne to come with her. Vivienne flushed a deep red and took in a few gulps of air before replying.

"Father, that may be a good idea, and I would be willing to go if that is alright with you."

"Vivienne", said her father, "you have always been a wise and prudent girl. Sometimes wise beyond your years. I trust you to make the right decision."

"Then it is settled." said Señor Carlos.

Maria rose from the table. "May I offer you a drink gentleman? We have some Papaya juice, or cool water from our stream, it comes straight from a source in the mountain".

"Water would be wonderful." said Señor Carlos, staring to feel the effects of the humidity. Victor Emanuel's eyes were on Vivienne as she stood and signaled to Lillianna to follow her to the bedroom. They hurried away to collect their items for the trip.

Meanwhile, Enrico who had been sitting in the cool comfort of the air conditioning in the car was feeling much better. He had removed his hat and combed his thick wavy hair. A woman who was perhaps in her fifties came close to him and looked in the window. She stood there for a while, peering through the windshield. Suddenly, she put her hand to her mouth as if in shock, smiled and waved as if in recognition, then ran away out of sight through the crowd that had gathered some twenty feet away. She returned about ten minutes later with another woman. A frail slim elderly woman with gray hair tied in a bun. She walked slowly but erect and the crowd parted to let her through.

Something in Enrico stirred, he felt his hair go taught at the roots. There was something strangely familiar about this woman. She stopped for a moment, one hand at her side, the other on her heart. Enrico swallowed hard. Emotions stirred within him, emotions which he had long thought ceased to exist. He stepped out of the car and stood holding onto the door handle. He pulled himself up to his full height, as tears welled up in his eyes. The woman walked forward and put her hand to her mouth.

"Enrico?" she said "Is, is that really you?"

"Yes Emilie. It is me." She stopped a few paces from him. He walked forward and took her in his arms. "Come my dear." he said, "Come with me, we have much to talk about." He opened the passenger door of the car and helped her into her seat.

Some thirty minutes later, Señor Carlos came out onto the deck by the stairs. He stood for a while looking over the many huts that dotted the terrain each side of the track. He turned and looked down onto the crowd that had gathered near his limousine, in time to see a thin elegant lady, perhaps in her seventies being helped out of the car by Enrico.

Chapter 6

Although the limousine had seating and comfort for many people, the trip back to the family home of Señor Carlos was not such a pleasant one. Conversation did not flow easily, and that which occurred was mostly in whispers. Señor Carlos occupied himself with his many reports, while Victor Emanuel read several newspapers. Occasionally while turning a page he would look across with a benign smile at the beautiful Vivienne who would instantly look down and flush with embarrassment. Fortunately for all concerned, the two young girls sat talking with the doll between them on another seat. The conversation was mostly one sided, with Donna Elaina, never at a loss for words, talking about her Paola, and how they passed their days together. When Lillianna spoke it was always in a whisper, whereupon, on one occasion, Donna Elaina said. "Speak up girl! No one is going to bite you!" They both started to laugh.

Finally they arrived before the entrance gates to the mansion. The old guard looked at Enrico and nodded, then pressed the button to open the wrought iron gates. He went back into his guard house and buzzed the main house to warn them of an immanent arrival.

By the time they had driven through the winding grove of trees to the front of the house, two maids were standing at the foot of the stairs waiting for them. They were dressed in black with white aprons and matching head pieces and came forward smiling to open the door and welcome the new arrivals. Señor Carlos stepped out of the car, briefcase in hand. As he walked up the stairs to the entrance, he motioned to his son to make arrangements for the new guests.

"Caterina! Take care of these young ladies. I suggest a room where they can sleep together." said Victor Emanuel. "One perhaps where there is a bathroom en suite."

Caterina waited for him to finish his discourse. "Sir Madame Di Caprio, in anticipation, has already suggested a room on our floor which has a double bed, with a bathroom. They will be very comfortable there. We will take good care of them Sir.".

Victor Emanuel smiled. Caterina was just a year younger than he. He knew where the vacant room was: He knew also where her room was, which she shared with another maid. They were next door to each other. As they spoke Vivienne looked at their faces. The smile that passed between them was not lost on her. He was tall dark and very handsome. He was also from a good family. The world was of his choosing and everything in it. She would take care not to be seduced by his charms, for like Caterina, his world and hers were far apart.

"Thank you Caterina", he said "Maybe later, when they are settled and have eaten, you could take them to the Arboretum."

"Yes Sir. It will be my pleasure." Victor Emanuel turned on his heels and was gone.

Caterina asked Lillianna and Vivienne to follow her and she went to the side of the main stairway and walked down a corridor to the end. She pushed open the double doors to allow Vivienne who was carrying two suitcases, to pass. Lillianna followed, her crutch making loud noises on the marble floor. Once through the doors, they came upon an elevator in front of them. At the side was a fairly narrow set of oak stairs that wound around in front of the elevator. Behind the stairs were two large doors with frosted glass windows. The windows had chicken wire in them. This then, was the staff entrance. "Normally we are not allowed to use the freight elevator unless we are moving heavy equipment." said Caterina walking over to the elevator door. "But in this case it will be alright and so much easier for the little girl as we are going up two floors." She pressed on the button and the elevator doors opened. The elevator was very large, almost like a small room. "We use this to move furniture and beds to the main bedrooms of the house. We are on the floor above them."

"How long have you been here?" said Vivienne? The maid looked briefly toward the ceiling before replying.

"About two years now. Why do you ask Madame?"

"It must be wonderful living in these conditions."

Caterina turned to face the two girls as they arrived

at the third floor and the doors slid open. "It is, and I cannot complain. It's just that it is a little lonely sometimes. I mean, we don't go into town very often. Well here we are. Your room is the third door down there on the left. I think you will like it. I will leave you here and will come for you in two hours when we will eat lunch. There is a refrigerator in your room. Please help yourself to anything inside, and take advantage of the bath and shower. I will see you later. Goodbye."

Vivienne and Lillianna knocked at the third door down the corridor. There was no reply, so they walked in. The room was small but well decorated. It had a double bed against the wall, a dresser and a chest of drawers upon which sat a small radio and a door to a walk in closet. Opposite, a small refrigerator was placed next to the table beside the window which overlooked the driveway, where they had driven up when they first arrived. In the distance they could just see the roof where the guard sat at the main gate.

"Let's look at the bathroom, said Vivienne. I would die to relax in a bath, like the one I have in that picture pinned up above my bed at home." They went to the bathroom. It was a long narrow room with a little window at the far end, also facing the front of the house. It was a little too high for Lillianna to see out.

The bath was large deep and old fashioned with legs that looked like lions paws with balls under them. It could be accessed from all sides save the end where the fixtures were, and these were against the far wall. Vivienne squealed with delight. She ran over to the bath, turned a mechanism to block the drain and opened up the faucets.

Water poured from both the hot and cold openings. Next to the bath was a chair upon which were several varieties of shampoos and soaps, and a bottle of fragrant lavender oil. She quickly unscrewed the lid and let several drops of oil fall into the water. The room was filled with the scent of lavender. "You can't believe how many nights that I have dreamed of doing this, and thanks to you my little Lillianna I am going to realize my dream." She walked over and kissed Lillianna on both cheeks and gave her a hug.

Lillianna laughed as Vivienne squeezed past her at the door. She left the room and in no time at all, returned completely naked. Lillianna looked at Vivienne's long slender body curved like that of a woman. She looked beautiful as she stepped into the bath her black hair, straight and shining hanging down her back almost to her waist. "Vivienne, she said, "How long will it be before I will be beautiful like you?"

"You are already very, very beautiful Lillianna."

"No I'm not, I can never be really beautiful, but how long will it be before I will have a chest?"

Vivienne laughed and blew bubbles as she sunk down below the foamy water. She pushed her hair back from her face, and came to the surface. "Lillianna, I can tell you now, that one day you will be the most beautiful lady of us all, and I'm not lying. Now, to answer your question, you are eight or almost. In two to three years you will have a chest. You will see, but don't be in such a hurry to grow up my darling!"

Lillianna sat on the edge of the chair. "When you have finished, please don't drain the water away. I know that we both took baths this morning, but I still would like to step in after you!"

At about 12.50 pm, there was a knock at the door. It was Caterina. "Are you ready to come and eat my ladies?" she said. The two girls were sitting on the bed in the same clothes they had worn earlier. These were their Sunday clothes and the best that they had. Lillianna was so happy that Sandra, who was a year older, had given the dress to her, only last week. They left the room. Lillianna felt a damp patch under her right arm. She had washed the crutch and it was still a little wet. "You ladies smell so nice," said Caterina, as she pressed the elevator button. The doors glided open and they walked in.

The kitchen was very large and there were silver tureens and plates stacked on a side table where a man in his latter years was busy cleaning them. He had removed his coat and starched collar, and was sitting at the end of the table with his sleeves rolled up. He nodded to them as they came in. The main table was wooden and very long. Probably twenty people could sit around it at one time. The places were all set and food was being put on the table.

Several women were seated at the table as others came in, followed by four men. The man who had been cleaning the silverware went to the sink and washed his hands. He returned to his chair and replaced his collar and tie that was hanging loosely from the back of the chair. He rolled down his sleeves and buttoned his cuffs, then returned and sat down at the head of the table. Each side of him sat a maid dressed in black with white lace around their necks, and on their sleeves, white cuffs. These ladies had white hair and were obviously senior household staff. Next to these, others took their places. Sometimes there were gaps between them. The four men were last in the seating arrangement. They were young and probably were the grounds men. Two unoccupied seats, midway down the table were shown to Lillianna and Vivienne. They walked to them and sat down.

A bell rang and the head man asked for all to bow their heads in prayer. After a few moments of silence he looked up. It was the signal for food to be passed along the table. The two visitors took a little of everything that passed before them and soon their plates were full of Chicken, Pork, vegetables yams and berries, which they covered in a sauce. They watched the others, and ate as they had never eaten before. Before long plates were taken and others; clean ones, arrived. It was Sunday, and so a special plate arrived with a layered ice cream cake. The maid next to Vivienne murmured that this was made in the kitchen, but only on Saturday evenings as it took too long to prepare. There were also cakes, and plates of biscuits on the center of the table and large steaming pots of coffee. It was an experience that neither girl would ever forget. Again the maid spoke in hushed tones. "We work hard here but the food is always good." One of the head maids, the one sitting diagonally across from her further up the table, stared at her through cold dark eyes. The maid fell silent, her cheeks becoming red, and she looked down at her plate.

Caterina entered the room. She had obviously eaten earlier, because she didn't sit down. She walked over to where Vivienne and Lillianna were seated. "Did you eat well, my ladies?"

"Very well thank you Caterina, it was excellent." said Vivienne.

"Good. Well this is the plan for today and tomorrow. I will leave you to rest in your room until four, when we will visit the Arboretum. After that we will have an evening meal at about six. pm, a little early I'm afraid, but the Master eats at 7 pm on Sundays as we all will attend Mass at 8 pm. Tomorrow morning you will receive breakfast in your room. And then at 9.30, Lillianna, you will go to the library where a doctor will come to fit you for your new leg."

Vivienne looked at Lillianna. "I can hardly believe it Lillianna. You will be able to walk after a little practice, with both legs, and you will be free to carry things with both hands, its wonderful news!"

Tears welled up in Lillianna's eyes. "I have so often dreamed of this, but never thought that it would happen." she said, and walking over to Caterina, threw her arms around her and hugged her.

Caterina's eyes filled with tears. "But it is not me little one, who makes this gift for you, It is the Di- Caprio family. Especially Miss Donna Elaina, who is so grateful to you for returning her doll to her, in fact it is because the doll lost a leg, though we don't understand why, that you are here."

"It is the Princess Camille who did this for me," said Lillianna, under her breath. Vivienne and Lillianna left the room, with the sound of Lillianna's crutch echoing on the marble floor, as they walked down the corridor to the elevator.

Chapter 7

At precisely 4 pm there was a knock at the door. Vivienne, who had been sitting on the bed, her hair combed and shining, crossed the room swiftly and opened it. It was a maid that she had not seen before. "Excuse me Miss, but I have been sent to take you to the Arboretum." she said.

"Oh thank you! My name is Vivienne, and this is my little sister Lillianna who is lying before you asleep on the bed. I will go and wake her up, and Oh please come in!" Lillianna was in a deep sleep. That which had taken place in the last few hours had overwhelmed her and had simply been too much for her.

The maid entered as Vivienne shook Lillianna from her torpor. Lillianna awoke, rubbed the sleep from her eyes and slipped off the side of the bed. She hopped over to the bathroom, washed her face and ran a comb through her hair. She took her crutch and came out of the room smiling. The three of them left the room and walked down the corridor to the elevator.

Once downstairs, they walked in front of the Grand Entrée to the library. Turning left they continued down a wide corridor with dark wood paneled walls on each side. On the left they passed in front of a set of double doors with a cross above the entrance. Further down the corridor they came upon another set of doors on the left. The maid opened one door, and they walked through it into an enclosed courtyard with a roof of glass. There were many chairs situated in rows in front of them, which could have doubled as a room for music recitals or simply seating for a lecture. At the far end behind the rows of seats, a wide stone staircase with railings on either side led to the Arboretum, and there in front of the door stood Victor Emanuel, casually dressed in a shirt rolled up at the sleeves and a pair of tweed trousers. Even in these clothes he had a distinguished look. He carried a notebook under his arm. The maid, who was leading the two girls, turned towards them, bowed her head and was gone.

"Ladies." he said, "I've taken the liberty of showing you around this indoor menagerie. It is one of my favorite places, and I come here quite often". The two girls descended the stairs and walked towards the entrance. He was smiling and gracious, as he explained that they would go through the first glass door and wait for it to close before opening the second one. Once on the other side, the humidity hit them like a blast. It was a question of leaving the dry air conditioned comfort of the mansion for the outside air, though all was enclosed in glass.

They walked down a stone slab pathway between

thick foliage that encroached upon them from both sides, into a clearing where there were park benches in an open area with a fairly large pond. The pond had an island of rocks at its center, from which water flowed over flat slabs past a small opening and down into the pond. Several turtles were lazing in the afternoon suns rays which shone through panes of a green glass dome at some height above. The pond had many colored fish which swam and played in the tepid water among the rocks.

Off to one side was a stand of palm trees which formed an alley to another area. They walked between these until they came to a large aviary, where birds of many varieties and colors flew from one branch to another in the trees around the edge. The birds may have been caged, but they had plenty of room to glide. Here too was a waterfall, but more spectacular than the last, dropping some twenty feet, and sending up a fine mist as it crashed onto the rocks below. Walking by the aviary they passed along a trail which took them back through many rows of exotic flowers and shrubs to the opening where benches were placed in position near the pond.

"Let us sit here for a moment." said Victor Emanuel. Vivienne and Lillianna sat down and Victor Emanuel drew up a seat facing them with his back to the pond. "Ladies, I hope that you have been well taken care of. Please let me know if there is anything that you need."

"No sir. I am most grateful for what you are doing for my little sister." said Vivienne.

Victor Emanuel smiled looking Vivienne in the eyes. "I would be most happy if you would call me Victor, Vivienne." Vivienne flushed and looked down at her feet. She was ill at ease in his presence. He turned towards Lillianna "I am interested to know more about you Lillianna. Are you really Vivienne's little sister?"

"No, I am not Sir, but they are the only family that I have." Lillianna stared directly at him, as he had done to Vivienne. This time it was he who looked away for an instant.

Victor Emanuel continued a puzzled expression upon his face. "My sister told me that you were living alone, I find that hard to believe!"

Vivienne interrupted. "Lillianna has always been very independent. When her mother died she came to live with us, but she wanted to live nearer the landfill so that she could take care of herself. She promised us though, that if ever she received another leg she would move back with us. We have taken her at her word, and so we are very happy about this event in our lives."

"You have a wonderful family Vivienne, and I'm sure Lillianna will be happy with you." said Victor Emanuel. His eyes appeared to glisten and he continued his conversation with Lillianna. "Lillianna, do you have a father? What is your family name?"

"I don't know sir." Lillianna stuttered.

Vivienne spoke. "I remember when Lillianna and her mother came to our village. She was a small baby of a little over one year. My mother told me that Lillianna's mother was fleeing from something and that she had a mysterious illness. She lived for a while hovering on deaths door before succumbing to her illness. Before she died she begged us to look after Lillianna, which we promised to do."

"Excuse me for asking you all of these questions," said

Victor Emanuel, "but I would like to be of help if I could. Do you know her family name, perhaps Vivienne?"

"My parents did ask her mother, but she never would say."

"That's very sad! Well, fate has brought both of you to us, and we are most happy that it did. Tomorrow you will have a new leg, which you will keep until you are eighteen, at which time you will have a permanent one fitted."

"Thank you Sir. I am very grateful. It will change my life." said Lillianna.

"Don't thank me. I believe you should thank, what was the name that you gave to the doll?" Lillianna bowed her head. She looked at Vivienne, who nodded.

"Go on. Say her name!"

"It was The Princess Camille," she said with some embarrassment.

"That is a beautiful name, I like it very much!" exclaimed Victor Emanuel. "I shall talk to her through the years, and whenever you are in need of help, I believe she will tell me.

Oh, there is something that I must do while you are seated there Lillianna. I would like you to remove your shoe and stand on this piece of paper I want to draw an outline of your foot so that we may phone the doctor, who will come tomorrow, with your correct foot size. Remember from tomorrow on you will be wearing two shoes."

Lillianna stood on the paper and he traced a pencil line around it. "Now off you go!" he said picking up the note book and putting it on the seat. Lillianna smiled a big smile and sat on the seat to put her shoe back on. Placing her crutch under her arm, she went off to look at the Parrots who were sitting on their posts further down the path around the bend.

"Thank you, Sir for being so very kind to her." Vivienne said "This is, without doubt, the greatest moment of her life. You have made her very happy. She chose the name Camille for the doll, because that was the name of her mother. It is so sad."

"Yes it is very sad, and it gives me great pleasure to know that this courageous little girl will be looked after by you from now on."

Vivienne's smile turned to a frown. "There is something that she doesn't know, something that we have never told her and perhaps I should not be telling you."

"Oh!" he said turning to face Vivienne. She was radiant and had a pure beauty which seemed to come from within. But now her brow was furrowed and her eyes were riveted on Lillianna in the distance. "What is it?" he said holding her hand and looking earnestly into her face. "What is it?" he insisted a second time.

"She must never know?"

"I promise that she will never know from me" he said earnestly.

"Well, her mother arrived at the steps to our house early one the morning. She told us that she had hidden, with her baby, in a Dumpster truck from the city the night before, and had stayed there until morning, when the truck left the city and had emptied its contents onto the landfill".

Vivienne's eyes misted over as she contemplated how difficult and agonizing it must have been for Camille, and how courageous she had been in her final hours. She felt

Victor Emanuel's hand squeezing hers and came out of her trance. She apologized for her lapse and continued. "She crawled with baby Lillianna along the path from the land fill to our home, as it was the closest. She did not die from a mysterious disease as I had said earlier. She died from a bullet wound to the chest!"

"A bullet wound!" he said, his eyes wide open.

"Yes! She was feverous and would not say what had happened to her. She was too afraid to even tell us her last name. All that she could do was to beg my mother to take care of her baby. She died in my mothers arms! I remember that it was at a time when there was fighting in the streets and an attempt to overthrow the government. I was probably about ten or eleven and knew little about it."

"Yes I was about the same age, or maybe just a few years older, and I remember that it had been a time of fear and uncertainty for our family also. You say that her mother's name was Camille?" Victor Emanuel stroked his chin looking pensively at his other hand in his lap.

"Yes! And her daughter's name is of course Lillianna." said Vivienne. "That could be useful too!"

Victor Emanuel sat deep in thought for a while, still holding Vivienne's hand in his. "What you tell me is hard to contemplate. "I feel so sad for you, and for Lillianna."

Suddenly he looked at his watch He breathed in quickly. "Please forgive me, but I have something to do before I go to dinner and so I must go now. Thank you for sharing your secret with me, I shall tell no one, not even my family, thank you also for the pleasure of your company this afternoon. Please stay here as long as you wish". As he stood up, he took his writing pad from the seat opposite.

He waved to Lillianna, who was returning from her visit to the parrots, and he was gone.

Vivienne sat there, her heart pulsing. Victor Emanuel was a strikingly handsome young man, but he was young, probably only two or three years older than she as he had said. He was cultured and had the benefit of a good education. Men of his kind usually married when they were in their mid thirties, and before that time had many lovers. She reaffirmed her decision, that she would be strong and not waiver to any advances that he may make. She laughed at her self. He had held her hand that was all. He had hardly made any advances. Lillianna arrived. So deep was Vivienne in her thoughts that she had not heard the sound of the crutch on the stone slab as she made her way towards her.

"Why are you laughing?" said Lillianna.

"I'm laughing because I'm happy. I am happy because tomorrow you will have a new leg, and you will come to live with us." Lillianna looked very serious.

"Vivienne, I need your help very much. Please don't laugh at me for what I'm about to say!"

"No, I won't; I promise my little flea. When you have such a serious face, I would never laugh at you. Now what is it?"

Lillianna took a seat next to Vivienne and looked up earnestly into her eyes. "Well, your father has collected so many books from the landfill, books on everything in the world."

"Yes that is true, mother laughs at him. He has books on subjects that he will never study, and he catalogues them all, putting each book in its own section. They fill up the whole wall of our living room as you know, but still he brings more into the house, we don't know where to put them. I'm sorry, I'm rambling, what is it that you wanted to ask me?"

"I want you to teach me to read. I want to study everything. I want to read every book in your house. Please don't laugh at me! Will you help me?"

Vivienne took her hand and kissed her on the cheek. "Of course I will my precious little one. We will start as soon as you move into our home, I promise you."

Lillianna put her arms around Vivienne and squeezed her tightly." I am so happy." she said "I shall never forget this moment!".Tears filled her eyes and her lips trembled as she managed to say in a high pitched voice before sobbing loudly. "I'm so happy, and grateful that you came with me to share it." Vivienne choked with emotion, ran her hand through Lillianna's hair.

"And I shall never forget this moment either my Lillianna!"

Chapter 8

THE BELLS CHIMED LOUDLY for vespers, and maids who were sitting around the kitchen table drinking coffee at the end of the evening meal jumped up and started to prepare for communion. "You will probably not need to go!" said a maid sitting near Lillianna and Vivienne.

Behind her stood one of the senior staff, the women who had looked upon them with narrow black eyes at lunch time. "Everybody needs to go!" she said in a loud voice, her hands placed firmly on each hip. She looked down upon the two young visitors seated at the table.

Vivienne handed Lillianna her crutch. "Come my little one, she said, Let us go!"

As they walked out into the corridor they were joined by a throng of maids and man servants all walking in the general direction of the library.

The door of the library was slightly open, and Vivienne could see the Di Caprio family assembled inside. Madame

Di Caprio was dressed in black with a black veil upon her head. She was sitting on a chair next to the large table with her hands clasped in her lap. Her eyes were closed; her face beautiful and serene. Her husband Señor Di Caprio was standing dressed in evening clothes reading a magazine article. They passed by the door and down the corridor into a magnificent chapel off to the left. Many candles shone brightly at the altar above which there was a beautiful wooden carving of Christ upon the cross. He looked down with sorrowful eyes upon the congregation. Each side of the altar, were stained glass windows which must have been illuminated by lighting from the outside, for the sun had long since sunk below the horizon. Lillianna was humbled by the beauty of it all, and moved, head bowed, to a seat nearby proffered by a maid who handed them little white lace doilies to place upon their heads.

All became quiet for about two minutes. Then the Di Caprio family moved silently down the aisle, the Señor, his wife on his arm, leading. He stood at the end of the aisle and watched his children passing in ascending order. Finally his wife took her place and he moved in beside her. After a few moments the priest appeared and the service began.

Lillianna's eyes glistened as she watched the rituals of the service taking place. Sitting there at the rear of the chapel, she was not able to see everything in front of her, but she could see the priest and the two little altar boys who worked in unison with him. She saw light glancing off the golden ornaments and the statue of Jesus looking down from his cross under the dark beams of the roof onto the small congregation, whose solemn pious faces were caught in the soft glow of candles that lit the altar and the aisles of the chapel. She was moved beyond words and squeezed the hand of Vivienne sitting beside her.

The Di Caprio's, led by Señor Di Caprio, rose and walked to the altar to receive the host. These were followed by the senior staff and in turn the rest of the congregation. Vivienne left her pew squeezing Lillianna's hand as she did so, she bent low and made the sign of the cross before joining the line.

Once back in their seats, everyone rose as the Di Caprio's walked down the center aisle and exited the chapel. Victor Emanuel turned towards Vivienne, bowed his head slightly and smiled as he passed by, leaving Vivienne flushed and looking down at her feet. The two girls walked out along the corridor passed the library where the family had gathered behind closed doors. They took the freight elevator to the second floor and walked in silence to their room.

Chapter 9

Lillianna was still asleep when a maid knocked and entered the room carrying a breakfast tray. Vivienne jumped from the bed and hastened to help place the tray upon the table. The maid wished her a good morning and hoped that she had slept well; she left abruptly. Lillianna wakened by the conversation sat up in bed. She could smell the strong aroma of coffee and saw the pastries and fruit on the tray.

"What an unbelievable way to wake up." she said to Vivienne. "Imagine, there are some people who wake up this way every day."

"It is true my little one, but for everyone who does there are thousands upon thousands who don't!"

"Vivienne, I'm going to be one of those people when I grow up." said Lillianna, whose dark eyes stared blankly into space.

"That's good my baby, but the first step is to get you

fitted for a new leg, and this we must do this morning. So hurry now and eat your breakfast, we have an appointment at nine thirty in the library." Vivienne turned away from Lillianna and went to the table." I must hurry too, if I want to take one more bath before I leave!"

Vivienne poured herself a coffee and disappeared with it into the bathroom. Lillianna pushed herself to the edge of the bed, reached for her cane and stepped onto the floor. She picked up a pastry and a glass of fruit juice. And set them beside her at the table. The bath water had stopped running and she heard Vivienne stepping into the water. She walked to the door and knocked on it. "Vivienne, please save the bath water for me!" she said.

"Alright my little flee, I shall. You may come in any time."

At nine thirty, Vivienne knocked on the library door and the two girls entered. Donna Elaina was sitting at the large table in the center of the room, holding her doll Paola, which was sitting on the table in front of her. Lillianna smiled and waved first to Donna Elaina, then to Princess Camille. She was happy to see her little baby again even though she was in the arms of someone else. Camille eyes glistened and seemed to smile back at her. At the end of the table sat a man, tall and lean with spectacles on the end of his nose. He had very little hair on the top of his head but it was still black. He rose and walked towards them. Vivienne introduced herself and Lillianna to the man in the dark suit.

"I am the Doctor Sanchez." he said "And you must be little Lillianna. Good. Well Lillianna. Let's get started. First I want you to remove your dress and shoes so that I can measure your whole leg. This will give me an idea of your expected growth in the next few years." Lillianna removed her dress and stood there in her underwear. She was very thin and her ribs showed clearly under a taught dark skin. "Now Lillianna I want to point out to you that first, this will not hurt you in any way, and second, there will be a short period of adjustment until you get used to your new leg, finally; this is not a pretty leg as such, not like the one you will have when you are fully grown. However, it will allow you to function well and you will come to like it." Vivienne who was holding Lillianna's dress walked over to a chair at the table and turned it to face out into the room. She sat down and smiled at Lillianna.

The Doctor Sanchez opened his black bag and started to take dimensions from Lillianna's foot to the socket at her hip on her good leg. Then from the socket to her knee joint. Finally he measured her foot. "You know young lady; I predict that you will be quite tall when you are fully grown." he said. "Yes, quite tall. I understand that you are about eight years old now. Is that right?"

Vivienne who had taken Lillianna's crutch from her spoke. "Yes we estimate that she is close to eight years old."

"Then you are not a relative?" said the doctor raising his eyebrows and looking over his glasses.

"No, but my family adopted her when she was just a little baby of about a year or more old, so she has become my little sister." The doctor inquired no further. He had become accustomed to too many stories such as Lillianna's to ask for further information.

"And I was just going to say how both of you are so

much alike." He smiled and Vivienne was surprised to see that he had blue eyes. He looked at his notebook and a chart that he had placed on the table nearby, and started to make some calculations. "Well I think that you are in luck Lillianna. I brought a pair of shoes with me. As instructed by Señor Di Caprio and based on conversations with his son, they should fit. Until that moment Vivienne and Lillianna had not seen a large box on the floor, out of view, behind the table.

The Doctor went over to the box with his note pad in his hand. Donna Elaina rose from her seat and took her doll with her.

"Come my Paola, I want you to see you what transpires here; maybe you too will get your leg back." So saying, she walked over and sat beside Lillianna. "Well Lillianna, for you this must be quite an exciting moment."

"Yes Miss Donna Elaina, a moment that will change me forever. May I hold your baby for a few moments?"

"I think that it would be an excellent idea Lillianna. I want my Paola to see everything. After all, it is because of her that we are all met here this morning!"

The Doctor pulled a sample leg from his box and referring to his note pad started making some adjustments. The leg was pink and ended above the knee where large leather straps hung unattached. He shortened the lower part of the leg. The foot had already been adjusted one size larger than Lillianna's foot size.

He came over to the chair where Lillianna was sitting, and slid the upper portion onto her thigh. "Now these straps will bind at first but your leg will get used to them. He turned to Vivienne. "Vivienne! It is Vivienne isn't it?"

"Yes Doctor, it is."

"Well Vivienne I am going to give you this tool. Your father or someone in the family will periodically need to adjust the lower limb and foot as Lillianna grows taller. Now Lillianna would you put the doll down for a moment?"

Lillianna held Camille close to her and kissed her hard on the cheek. She whispered in the dolls ear.

"Thank you so much my guardian angel I shall never forget what you have done for me." The doll seemed to blink and smile imperceptibly, though certainly enough for Donna Elaina and Lillianna to see. Donna Elaina took the doll and set her on her lap facing Lillianna.

The doctor produced a pair of shoes unlike any that Lillianna had seen before. They were beautiful red leather shoes, with little tags at the back to make putting them on easier. "Here put this one on." he said. And he in turn fitted the other to the artificial limb. The leg was not as pretty as Lillianna had thought she was expecting something better. It really did look artificial.

The Doctor saw the disappointment in her eyes. "Lillianna" he said. "This artificial limb is probably not quite as you expected. You probably thought that it would look like a real one. Well I can promise you two things. The first is that you will grow to love it as you will be able to do so much more. And second. The limb that you will receive when you are fully grown will be difficult to tell from your real leg."

"Sir, said Lillianna I am already most grateful for what everyone is doing for me. I assure you I will be very happy with this one. And if I am lucky enough to get another when I am grown then I will probably be too attached to this one to throw it away."

The Doctor looked across at Vivienne and then back at Lillianna. "You are a remarkable young lady Lillianna. Mature beyond your years. I have done hundreds of such fittings but you are certainly a rare one. Now let's see if we can walk on it, and don't be discouraged if it doesn't feel too good right now. I can assure you that it will. Please use your crutch at the same time until you can discard it."

Lillianna stood up and started to walk around the room. It felt odd at first, but slowly she began to trust it more and more until finally she let the crutch fall to the ground. The doctor clapped his hands. "Bravo!" He said. "I've seen people do well with two artificial limbs. Bravo!"

Lillianna put her dress on and stood admiring herself in the mirror. "It's going to be alright." she said, as Vivienne stood up and clapped. Tears were streaming down her face as she ran over to Lillianna and threw her arms around her.

"My courageous little one, I love you so much." she cried, sobbing on Lillianna's shoulder

There was a knock on the door and Victor Emanuel entered. He was dressed formally and nodded to Vivienne as he spoke "My father sends his apologies Doctor. He is very busy this morning and has already left the house. He has asked me to come on his behalf."

"That's fine young Sir, I am finished here. If you would send some men to put this box in my car, then I will leave and send you my honoraria later."

"That will be fine Doctor. I'll have your bags removed

immediately, and thank you so much for having come at such short notice."

The Doctor busied himself preparing to leave. Victor Emanuel left the room and returned with two men. They picked up the doctor's box and left the room.

"Now Vivienne." said Victor Emanuel, "I would like to come from time to time if I may, to see how Lillianna is doing. Perhaps I could pick you up and bring you into the city."

"A trip to the city would be nice for us. Thank you." said Vivienne. Victor Emanuel felt uncomfortable. He was used to young women falling at his feet, especially those of limited means. Vivienne was different, seemingly uninterested, and he didn't know how to handle the situation. He just felt that he would like to see her again. He rung a bell and Enrico appeared.

"Enrico; take these ladies back to their village. I believe they have some cases in their room."

"I will take care of it Sir." said Enrico.

"And Enrico, I won't be requiring you again this morning. My father tells me that you may have a friend in the village. Please take your time."

"Thank you sir." said Enrico bowing his head in respect.

"Now ladies, I will take my leave of you. I have enjoyed having you here in my home." He shook hands with both of them and left the room.

The girls returned to their room, Lillianna walking with the aid of her crutch on her new leg. It was a bitter sweet moment for them as they looked around the room for the last time, making sure that they hadn't left anything behind. While Vivienne busied herself with their suitcases, Lillianna took the bar of soap they had washed with in the bath, and slipped it into her pocket. It smelled so good, better than anything that she had ever used and while she new that Vivienne would not condone her taking it, but she would certainly be happy using it in the tub near the kitchen sink.

There was a knock on the door; Enrico arrived for their cases. They walked around the two rooms looking under the bed to make sure that they had not left any of their meager possessions behind, and followed him down the corridor. They took the elevator to the ground floor and walked along the hallway to the Grand Entrée. None of the family was present, and the entrance was deserted except for the maid who had befriended them in the kitchen. She came forward and shook their hands, wishing them a safe journey, looking around as she did so. Enrico led the way out of the entrance and down the stairs to a large sedan. It was not the limousine which had been used to take Señor Di Caprio into town with the other driver, but just the same it afforded great comfort and had a partition between the chauffeur and passengers and two seats facing rearwards.

The road home was a somber one. The two girls sat, hardly talking, each in her own reverie. Enrico occasionally glanced at them through his rear view mirror. He had seen much in over fifty years of driving for three generations of the Di Caprio family. He remembered Señor Carlos as a little boy and had been his confident into manhood, but he kept everything to himself, never revealing anything of his conversations with any of the household staff. He was a trusted and loyal servant who had given his life to the service of one family. In return, he had a small air conditioned apartment above the garage, regular meals with the staff in the kitchen, and a job, which for the most part allowed him, a fair amount of free time. Although his salary was small, he had little need for much money and over the period of fifty years had invested his savings wisely. As a result, he had amassed a small fortune, for a man in his situation.

Soon they had left the main streets of town and were heading along familiar lanes to the village. The road was rough and unpaved, but Enrico was a good driver and he was able to avoid the occasional dip in the road. Finally they arrived at their destination in front of Vivienne's home. A crowd had gathered as before. Enrico removed their luggage from the trunk and carried it up the stairs to the entrance of their home. He returned as Lillianna stepped out of the car. She walked slowly, without the aid of her crutch. Enrico stood at the foot of the stairs. He removed his hat and bowed his head and said. "Good luck my ladies" Lillianna walked towards him and hugged him, burying her face into his waist followed by Vivienne who kissed him on his cheek. He seemed immobile and showed no sign of emotion. Years of service to others had done that to him, had made him transparent, imperceptible, as he opened car doors, picked up luggage and bowed his head, esteeming all superior to himself. He nodded slowly several times, put his cap back on his head, turned and walked towards the car.

Lillianna grasped the handrail looking into the eyes of curious faces above. She held their gaze, as slowly she pulled herself up the stairs, smiling from ear to ear. The family, waiting at the top, clapped their hands, Maria laughing through her tears came forward, her arms outstretched, as Lillianna stood proudly at the top of the stairs with her hands on her hips. Alfredo ran down the steps to help Vivienne with the cases, and the crutch, which Lillianna had left behind. Maria took Lillianna in her arms and hugged her, sobbing loudly. They rocked from side to side for some time before Maria could gather herself long enough to speak. "Now my little one." she said. "Come inside and tell me all about your adventure.

By the time Enrico returned to the car, a small crowd had gathered, and word had passed among the villagers that Lillianna and Vivienne were back. It wasn't long, as Enrico had hoped, before the crowd parted, to allow passage for the tall frail elegant woman with the bun. He had thought of little else since their last meeting a few days earlier. "Emilie!" He said in a voice chocked with emotion. "Come, my dear." He reached for her hand. "Come into the car. I must talk to you!" He took his hat off and held her hand as he helped her into the passenger's seat. Closing the door he walked around the back of the car and got into the drivers seat and closed his door. He started the engine and they glided through the crowd of well wishers out of the village to the trail beyond.

It was not until they were out of the village and on the road up the hill that he pulled into a side road and came to a stop. The view overlooked a valley dotted with individual homes surrounding a lake. They had high walls around them, but from the promontory the couple was able to see into them. For the most part they encircled small gardens of flowers and vegetables set against their walls, and with grassy areas in the center. There was an above ground pool in one, where a few children were gathered taking turns to jump into it. A dog was huddled in the shade of the pool taking advantage of the sprays of water that sometimes sloshed over the side. The couple sat hand in hand staring ahead and talking over times past in the cool air conditioned comfort of the car for probably an hour, before he reversed back onto the main track and returned to the village and dropped Emilie off. Squeezing her hands tightly in his, he looked deeply into her eyes, eyes that had misted over.

"You're still as beautiful as the day I first saw you." he said.

"And you, Enrico, you rest forever young."

He kissed her gently, and they held that embrace for a long time. He held her hands tightly for a moment longer and turned, a tall lean figure, walking erect back to the car. He got back into the drivers seat, adjusted his hat, He took one last look at her as he glided slowly away, watching Emilie waving to him in his rear view mirror as he drove up the hill. He kept his eyes fixed upon her as the image got smaller and smaller until she passed out of sight.

Chapter 10

Señor Di Caprio was sitting in his study just off the library when he heard a knock at his door. "Enter!" He said without looking up. Enrico stood before him, his hat in his hands.

"Ah, Enrico." he said. "Did you take care of the young ladies from the village?"

"Yes Sir. They asked me to thank you for all that you have done for them, and that they would never forget your kindness"

Señor Di Caprio adjusted himself in his seat He had a pen in his hand and a document before him. He looked at Enrico. "There is something else isn't there?" he said putting his pen down upon the table.

"Yes Sir, but I can come back when you are not busy."

"No, eh, now would be a good moment. Sit down, you look a little distressed."

Enrico thanked him and sat down, his hands moving

nervously around the brim of his hat. "Sir, I don't know where to begin. I....".

"Perhaps I can help you Enrico. I have been talking to my son recently. Does this have anything to do with your recent trips to that village? We noted that you were in conversation with a lady there. Did you perhaps see her again today?"

Enrico raised his head and stared at Señor Di Caprio's hands that were clasped before him on the desk. He seemed surprised.

"Yes sir. We grew up in the same village, not too far from here. I had always thought that we would marry, but when the time came, she married another. They had two daughters and I came here to be Señor Di Caprio senior's chauffeur. Fifty years have passed and I had often wondered what had become of her and her daughters. Somehow, one of her daughters recognized me when I went to this other village recently, and she told her mother, whom I think you saw when I drove you there a few days ago." Señor Di Caprio nodded, but did not speak. "Her husband died after they had been married for ten years and she was forced to move out of his home. She moved to that village where she was able to live off the landfill to support her daughters."

Enrico closed his eyes and looked down at his feet. The pain of the images that flashed by in his brain had been too much for him. "Sir, I am old now, and I would like to take the years remaining to me to protect her, and make her happy. She has seen too many years of misery!"

Señor Di Caprio pulled himself up in his chair. "Well Enrico. I hope that you are not asking for permission to leave us? I mean we would be lost without you. You are part of our family!"

"Yes Sir and I'm very grateful for the life that I've had here."

Señor Di Caprio rose from his chair and walked to the window. He clasped his hands behind him and looked out, rocking backwards and forwards on his feet.

"As you know, the rules here call for a single man as the principal chauffeur. These rules were made long ago and in principle I agree with them and would not change them. One of the reasons that this rule was instituted, as it is indeed for all of the household staff, is because of the inevitability of the arrival of children in a marriage. We could not afford to have children running all over the place. However in your case, this would not be a problem. Now if you were to marry, I see no reason why your wife should not move in with you, subject to my talking to the rest of the staff. You have been a loyal and trusted servant and have lived here longer than any of us."

Señor Di Caprio had a worried look upon his face. He walked back to his desk and sat down. He stared at Enrico. "I have always known that this day would arrive, but still, I need time to adjust to it. If you were able to guarantee me one more year of employment, it would give me time to find another chauffeur. To find another like you, whom I can trust, will take time, and frankly I doubt that such a man exists. You will need time also to find a home in another place and to adapt to your new surroundings."

Enrico stood up. "It is with the heaviest of heart that I come to you today Sir. I could see no way out of my situation and everything looked bleak, but I knew that whatever the cost I would pay it to be with my Emilie. I want to spend the years that remain to me trying to making her happy. Once again Sir you have made a seemingly impossible task, possible, and for that I am very, very, grateful."

"Good, said Señor Di Caprio, then we will proceed on those terms."

"Thank you Sir." said Enrico as he turned and left the room, his head held high, tears of joy welling up within him.

Chapter 11

SANDRA SAT WITH HER arms around Lillianna at the dining room table. "Lillianna, it's so good to have you back with us. I have plenty of room in my bed and we will have lots of fun growing up together."

Lillianna sat motionless looking at the books along the wall of the dining room. "I'm so happy to be living here." she said. "Vivienne told me that she is going to help me read and I'm going to read every book on that wall." Sandra laughed heartily.

Maria stood up. "Today we are truly blessed. We have two pieces of good news. The first, as you all know, Lillianna has come to live with us. And second, Papa has been promised work as a welder in a new plant under construction near here. The work will last several years and we may be moving closer to town and living in a real house. You know everything has changed since Lillianna found that doll on the landfill. I think that we should all hold our hands together and bow our heads in prayer." All the family moved closer together and bowed their heads, with the exception of Lillianna whose eyes remained fixed upon the books along the wall.

.......End of part one.

Part Two

Chapter 12

...TEN YEARS PASSED. ALFREDO had worked hard and skillfully as a welder and had been promoted to foreman. He moved constantly to where the work would take him, leaving his family behind in the three bedroom house closer to town where they had moved some nine years ago. Pedro had become a carpenter and had added another room on to the side of the house before going north to help build a huge housing estate close to a large city. Like his father he sent money home to support the family. He would come home from time to time but for the most part he had left home. All that remained at home were the five women. Sandra and Lillianna still shared a bedroom. They had become inseparable and complimented each other as they were totally different in character. Sandra was full of fun and outward going, while Lillianna was quiet, and liked nothing more than to sit and read a book in her bedroom She had been awarded the prize for top student in her class, and had been given a scholarship to a university by a group from a foreign country who had decided to sponsor her as a student, since her school magazine had written an article about her as the student with the most promising future. She had become so expert at walking, that people scarcely knew that she had an artificial leg. She wore long dresses and was able to use many of Vivienne's shoes, as Vivienne, who was working in the perfume section of a large department store, was able to buy shoes from the store at discounted prices.

Vivienne had fallen in love with an engineer who would come into the store to buy perfume for his mother. He bought many bottles of perfume, before he had the courage to ask Vivienne for a date. Lillianna or Sandra would take it in turns chaperoning their big sister, until the couple were engaged. At that time an arrangement was made whereby the girls would leave the house with Vivienne, and once clear of it would arrange for Vivienne to meet them later at a prearranged destination. To their extreme shock, Vivienne came in one night sobbing bitterly. Her boyfriend had been killed in a car accident. It would take her almost a year before she could recover enough to go to a café with her sisters. She absorbed herself in her work, and often volunteered to work on the weekends just to keep her mind from the pain that she felt inside. Lillianna owed her much, for it was she who had spent so many hours helping her with her studies.

Lillianna went on to college to study law, but she always remembered her roots and spent her weekends at home. It was one of these weekends when she was sitting chatting to Maria and Sandra that there came a knock at the door. Maria went to the door and was confronted by an elegant young lady with dark wavy hair, wearing the most expensive of clothes. Behind her a Chauffeur, a man in his forties, stood next to a large shiny black car.

"I am looking for a young lady by the name of Lillianna. Do you have anyone here of that name?" she said, her voice carrying through into the room.

Maria put her hand to her chest and said "Yes we do. Will you please step inside? Whom should I say is calling?"

"I am Donna Elaina Conseuiller Di Caprio, and here is my Card." she said, reaching into her designer hand bag and pulling out a card. Donna Elaina stepped inside the house. It was modestly furnished but in perfect order with everything in its chosen place. She walked over to the mirror beside the mantle and started to adjust her hair. She was fashionably dressed and wore dark nylon stockings and black patent leather high heel shoes. Without the shoes, her appearance would have been that of someone a little short, and slightly overweight.

Lillianna entered the room, and walked over to Donna Elaina, her arms outstretched. "My dear Donna Elaina," the words flowed easily from Lillianna's tongue, "How very nice to see you!" Lillianna, was almost a head taller than Donna Elaina, and would have hugged her had Donna Elaina not backed up in surprise.

"Lillianna, you have changed, much more than I could ever have imagined." she said, somewhat taken off guard. She proffered a hand and Lillianna shook it vigorously.

"Donna Elaina, you look absolutely beautiful. It's certainly a great pleasure to see you." Her brow began to furrow and she turned her head to one side. "But what is it that brings you to our home?"

Donna Elaina raised her hands in front of her, somewhat like a preacher confronting his congregation. "You won't believe what I am about to tell you Lillianna. Do you remember that silly little doll that I had called Paola" She didn't wait for Lillianna to speak. "Well something has happened of late which caused me to think of you. Paola has started to cry real tears again in the morning! I tried for days to fathom out why she was doing that. Then suddenly it came to me. I realized the promise that my father and I had made to you all those years ago, and that now you must be very close to eighteen."

Lillianna cupped her hands in front of her mouth. Her eyes widened and she took in a quick breath of air. So Princess Camille had remembered her. She felt her bottom lip start to quiver and her eyes misted over.

"Please allow me to finish!".Donna Elaina said, raising her hand. She was not in the habit of someone interrupting her mid point in her dialogue, especially someone of lower station. "I have spoken with my father Señor Di Caprio, and reminded him of that covenant we had many years ago with regard to you changing your prosthesis when you became of age. I want to tell you that this agreement still stands, and although I do not respond to the dictates of a mere doll, I am conscious of the troubles that have befallen my family over recent years and do not want further harm to come to them. So I am here to take you with me now to have a new limb fitted."

Lillianna regained her composure. Here was a cry for help from a young lady, who for all her bravado, was still the same little girl inside. She took a struggling Donna Elaina in her arms and squeezed her. As she did so Donna Elaina spotted the gold bracelet on Lillianna's right wrist.

"My god that is a beautiful bracelet!" she said. "However did you come by it?"

Lillianna looked at her in surprise. "Oh that. Well it is something I received last year from my family. You see it was my birth mother's, which my stepmother removed from her wrist after she had died. I never knew of its existence until last year when she gave it to me. She had been saving it for me all those years until I was old enough to appreciate it and not lose it. I think it was a gift from my father to her, because as you will see… At that moment she released the bracelet from her wrist, "It has an inscription upon it."

Donna Elaina took the bracelet and looked at it. It was indeed a fine piece of jewelry. She turned it over, and on its underside was the inscription. 'To C. Forever my love. B. Donna Elaina came close to tears. Lillianna, that is truly beautiful, you must never loose it. It is such a simple phrase, but it says everything."

"Well that was indeed fortunate." said Lillianna "As there wasn't any room for more." Both girls hugged each other and Donna Elaina laughed heartily.

"You are always able to make me laugh Lillianna." she said, wiping a tear from the corner of her eye. "Please say that you will come with me, now; I simply won't accept a negative reply."

Lillianna pulled herself away from Donna Elaina, and they stood holding each others hands. It was Lillianna who spoke. "I remember your generous offer of many years ago, but I don't think that it will be necessary now. By sheer coincidence, I recently made an appointment, with the same doctor, who came to your house some ten years ago, to measure me for my prosthesis. I should return next week to receive my new limb."

Donna Elaina was taken aback. "You were able to do this on your own?" She looked somewhat shocked and turned her head from side to side in disbelief.

"No my family is going to pay for it and I will refund them later."

She took hold of Lillianna's face between both hands, and pulled it down and close to her. Her eyes, wide open darted from one of Lillianna's eyes to the other "But you must allow us pay for the cost. I mean, we made that promise to you, you must remember!" Her former poise had left her and had been replaced by wide eyed terror. Lillianna took hold of her tenderly and gently held her to her breast.

Compassion welled up within her for this girl who seemed to have everything and yet was quite alone, and who, even now needed the love and affection of a doll to replace, in some measure, the loneliness felt by a woman born into a certain level of society where an open show of affection was frowned upon. "Please don't worry Donna, I can assure you that Princess Camille, I mean Paola; will be fine when you arrive in your house. You see, for her it was perhaps necessary for you to make the move; that is to come and see me, to fill your contract with her. You did that, and she will know it, and so now, all is fulfilled."

Suddenly Donna Elaina seemed like a little child. "But you will come and see her when you receive your new leg? And my father will take care of the costs. He needs to! You see he like me is quite superstitious." She paused, and looked around to see if there was anyone within ear shot who might hear her conversation. "What I'm about to tell you, you may find quite strange, perhaps even laughable, but my father and I believe that it is your mother who speaks to us through Paola. Paola has always been your guardian angel and it was she who made us aware of your plight, with unmistakable signs. That is why, not only should my father pay for your limb, but that it is in his interest to pay, and it needs to be the best limb money can buy. He would not be able to rest if he could not do this for you. I don't know what we would have done had you gone ahead and purchased one on your own. But then, you see Paola knew and she would not have allowed that to happen. It is of the utmost importance to me that Paola, my father, and I see you with your leg as soon as you can come to our home."

Lillianna, her voice calm, her eyes tenderly gazing into the wide searching eyes of Donna Elaina, spoke softly. "I will be happy to come and see you and Paola, when I receive my new leg. Now please don't worry and I promise that I will call you, Donna Elaina. Thank you so much for coming!".

Donna Elaina ran to Lillianna and put her arms around her. "Lillianna, we simply must remain friends and see each other much more often, now that we are older. Don't you see that we are inexorably linked? I have always felt relaxed with you and know that I can trust you. Please say that you will come and see us soon?" she said, her dark eyes darting wildly from side to side as she looked up again into those of Lillianna. "I am so excited and happy to have found you again. In memory of this meeting, I shall change Paola's name to that of Camille. Yes, Princess Camille, in honor of our friendship."

"Well we will see." said Lillianna; I like the name of Paola."

"No, it was Camille who brought us together." Donna Elaina lowered her head and set her eyes firmly. When she took this stance there would be no more arguments. "It will be Princess Camille!" They both laughed and hugged each other.

Donna Elaina walked out of the home, not turning back for fear that she would not be able to control her emotions. She skipped down the few steps to the limousine where the chauffeur waited by the open door. He returned to the drivers seat, started the motor, and they glided away, with Donna Elaina crying from behind tinted glass.

Maria came back into the room. "What is it that you have my darling Lillianna that lions in your presence become as lambs?"

"Whatever I have my dear Maria, I owe it to you. You took me in, gave me a family, and turned a frightened, proud, rebellious little girl into a loving caring daughter. I shall never forget what you have done for me. I am the most fortunate of young ladies" They hugged each other, their heads locked together, rocking from side to side for a long time.

Chapter 13

PEDRO WAS COMING HOME and the family was in a state of excitement. It had been almost a year since his last visit. Alfredo busied himself cutting away some brush at the front of the yard near the house. Maria looked out of the window and called to Sandra.

"You know, I've been asking your father to cut back those bushes for some time. He always told me that he was just too busy, but today his son is coming home and suddenly he has found time to do it, so that he will be the first to see Pedro when he turns the corner at the end of the road."

Sandra came to the window and put her arm around her mother. "And you mother, you must have cleaned that window at least three times!"Sandra was grinning from ear to ear. She was extremely thin and beautiful like her mother, but she had her father's deep expressive eyes and black curly hair, which she kept fairly short about her shoulders. She was wearing a pretty dress that Vivienne had bought for her, and she had recently found work in the same department store as Vivienne. There was talk that she would move in and share an apartment with Vivienne, but for now she was still staying at home.

A small pickup truck rounded the corner with two men seated in the cab and a third in the bed at the back. It stopped at the end of the street. The man jumped from the bed of the truck and removed his bag as another opened the door also removing his bag from beside him, leaving the driver at the wheel. They waved to each other as they left, each going in a separate direction. The truck moved closer. Alfredo shrieked with joy when he saw who was behind the wheel of the truck; it was Pedro smiling and waving. The truck came to a stop in front of the house and Pedro stepped out, lean and looking like his father, with the same way of walking, but almost a head taller. He ran around the car and the two men stood hugging each other for some time.

Maria stood in the doorway, a dish cloth in her hand, with Sandra right behind her, she felt dizzy with joy and her eyes fogged over. Pedro looked up at his mother and smiled. He leaped up the stairs two at a time and picked her up, squeezing her in his arms. Tears rolled down Maria cheeks as she kissed her son on his face and neck. He put his mother down and reached over and hugged his sister. She also was close to tears. They entered the house. Alfredo, suddenly finished with his chores, was close behind.

Pedro looked around him. "Where are Anita Vivienne

and Lillianna?" he said, putting his head in the kitchen doorway.

Maria put her hands on his back and made circular movements with them. "They are in town. They went to see Vivienne but should be back any time."

Pedro registered a look of surprised "You mean they knew I was coming and they went to town. Some kind of reception that is!".

"No my son, they went to town yesterday and stayed overnight at Vivienne's apartment. I shouldn't really tell you this, but Lillie is having her permanent leg fitted, and she wanted to surprise you. They will be here on the next bus which should arrive soon."

Pedro gestured to his father, his palms facing up waist high in front of him. "You mean we have a bus stopping here now?"

His father rubbed the back of his neck, holding his pipe with his free hand. "Yes, a bus does the trip into town two times a day; stops right at the end of the street!" A broad grin crossed his face revealing a mouth where several teeth were missing both on the top and bottom, but he had a good set of black shiny hair and his eyes twinkled and shone; he was still a handsome man.

"We are moving up in the world. That means that you can go into town shopping Momma!".

"Yes my son, it is true, but I still rely on your father to do most of the shopping. I don't like the noise of all that traffic."

Pedro walked to the kitchen. Two chickens were lying with their feet bound tightly together on the table close to the sink. They turned their heads in his direction and except for the occasional blinking of their eyes, lay motionless unaware of their fate. "God, I am so happy to be home," he said returning to the room.

Alfredo, who had gone out onto the porch turned to them and said in an excited voice. "Pedro, here they come!"

Pedro ran to the stairs and looked down the street. Three women were walking side by side, having just descended from the bus, which had turned left and was heading in the opposite direction. "I can't believe it!" he yelled. Anita is all growed up, and just look at Lillianna, she is walking so well on her new leg, and I would not be able to tell the difference. She too is so tall now, almost as tall as me. I can't believe it! Will you look at Vivienne; she looks as beautiful as ever and has all the grace of a fine lady." He took the stairs in two leaps, and ran along the road to greet them, picking each one up and swinging them in circles and kissing them on their cheeks. He was lean and tanned; his black wavy hair sparkled and shone in the noonday haze. Maria put her hand on her breast. She had so much to be proud of as she looked at all of her babies now so grown up.

Alfredo half sat on the rail with one leg swinging in the breeze. He started to light his pipe, a habit he had taken most recently though usually after the evening meal. He had a contented smile on his face and winked at Maria, who was now crying tears of joy. She walked over to Alfredo and kissed him lightly on the cheek. "Thank you, so very, very much, my darling!" she said. Alfredo put his arm around her, and continued to smile.

At the meal table, Pedro told them of his adventures

over the last year. He had everyone's attention, but none more so than Lillianna, whose eyes rested upon his face and every detail that came from his mouth. He spoke of the recent turn of events in the country. About General Armaldo, who had returned from sixteen years in exile, and how some of the old guard in the army had deserted with their men to join his ranks. How his number of supporters was growing more every day as he waited on the outskirts of the Capital city. How the president and his followers were becoming more and more alarmed by the situation and were trying to rally key members of the military to curb the insurrection.

"The situation looks tense and we could have another coup d'Etat in the next few weeks." said Pedro.

"Well the government has promised much and done little to assuage the terrible plight of the poor in our country." Lillianna was on her favorite topic. With only three years to go on her law degree, she was anxious to join the fight to help the oppressed, and was president of the 'Save Our People' forum on campus. "Aid comes to our country from other richer countries in the form of loans, and it ends up in the pockets of the politicians. It will always be this way, until, or unless a strong military leader takes power and puts these criminals behind bars, which is no less than they deserve" Her face had reddened and her eyes appeared to be staring into space. "I hope this General Armaldo is such a person! What is he like?"

"I haven't seen him," said Pedro, "but from what I've heard, he is a very big man, very tall, with white haired and a big moustache that grows right out onto his cheeks. They say that he has been in exile for many years, and that during that time he learned military tactics and was supported by large foreign powers. That is all I know about him. I don't know much about politics and care little about it. I don't think that we will see change in my lifetime so I don't worry as long as I can provide for my family."

Lillianna's eyes flashed, her face became taught. "Pedro this is precisely the problem. You must start to care! It's only by people caring that we can affect change in our country." Pedro smiled and looked down at his feet. "I'm sorry." she said. "I didn't mean to get so roused, especially on your first day home Pedro, but this is something very important to me."

"Let's change the subject." said Vivienne. "Donna Elaina Di Caprio telephoned me at my work this morning." Vivienne patted the back of her head and smiled. "The supervisor would have told me off, as phone calls are strictly forbidden, except in a dire emergency; or during the lunch break, where we may use a pay phone in the entrance. However, when a certain Donna Elaina Di Caprio said her name, the supervisor straightened right up and became most pleasant, from then on she was all smiles; Donna Elaina is a very good customer. I went over to the phone and I could see the supervisor looking at me green with envy as I chatted with her."

"What did she want?" said Maria, cupping her hand to her mouth, her eyes registering alarm.

"Don't worry Mama. She asks if Lillianna would come to see her tomorrow. She said that she had something to relate to her, that it was 'of relevance, and extremely important.' She is sending the Limousine here at around ten."

Pedro stood up and bowed very low, he brought his

hand down, practically sweeping along the floor as he held an imaginary hat. "Well excuse me Mademoiselle! I wonder if your ladyship isn't becoming too exalted for this company.".

Lillianna's eyes flashed. "Please don't talk to me like that, even in jest Pedro. You are the only family that I have and all that I will ever need. You mean everything to me and I will be here long after you have gone away and created a family of your own."

Pedro saw the look in her eyes and he felt a sudden tenderness towards her. It was as if he was seeing her for the first time, and he fought back an overwhelming desire to take her in his arms and kiss her. At that moment he felt so helpless. This was no longer his little sister, but a beautiful young princess whom he didn't know. In this last year, so much had changed. He could see that they were growing apart, and there was nothing he could do to stop it or narrow the gap. "I would be happy to take you tomorrow in my truck if you would like." He stammered and felt awkward. He wondered what was going on inside of him!

"Thank you Pedro that would be an honor, but I have no way of stopping the Limousine now. Perhaps you could pick me up though for the return trip, I shouldn't be very long at the Di Caprio's."

Maria looked across at Alfredo, and then at her son. Things were moving too fast for her. She had never considered Lillianna as anything but her daughter. Vivienne, as usual, came to the rescue.

"I am so hungry, why don't we prepare the lunch, and you Father, you told me that you have been waiting for Pedro to come home so that he could help you lift that heavy beam into place on the addition at the rear of the house."

The two men stood up, happy to seize the opportunity to get out of the house and do something together. Maria walked towards the kitchen followed by her daughters. The chickens were lying with their eyes closed. They opened them and shook their heads as they entered. It was time.

Chapter 14

Donna Elaina skipped down the steps at high speed, and stood waiting impatiently as the Limousine arrived. She waved to Lillianna, whom she could only make out as a dark shape in the rear of the car. The chauffeur stepped out and would have run around to open the door for Lillianna, had not Donna Elaina got there first. She was smiling, her teeth white and even, showed between sensuous red shiny lips, her eyes wide and shining in anticipation. "My dear Lillianna." she said almost breathlessly. "I'm so excited to see you. You will not believe your eyes! I can hardly contain myself."

Lillianna stepped out of the car effortlessly and embraced Donna Elaina. "What is it my dear? I have scarcely ever seen you so excited!"

Donna Elaina grabbed her hand and started to pull her up the stairs. "Come with me!" she said "You're not going to believe this!" They skipped up the remaining stairs together and were soon in the cool comfort of the main hall. They ran hand in hand to the library. Donna Elaina opened the door and they went inside.

Once inside the room Lillianna saw Princess Camille standing unaided in front of the bureau. "What do you think? It all happened two days ago. I swear it!"

"What happened?" Lillianna's brow furrowed.

"Well look at her, don't you see! She has two complete perfectly formed legs. And stranger yet, when I awoke yesterday, she was standing in my bedroom with her stockings and shoes on; both of them. I haven't seen the missing shoe and stocking for at least ten years. Don't you remember we searched everywhere in the bed for it; well anyway I did!" Donna Elaina was trembling as she took Lillianna's hand in hers. "It's a miracle Lillianna, and somehow it's all tied in with you. You have your new leg and she has hers."

Lillianna went to the doll, picked it up and stood it on the table. The doll's eyes were bright and shining and for a moment Lillianna thought that it was going to talk; so real was she. "I do not have an explanation for you Donna Elaina, except that it could be that one of your brothers or a maid who had removed the stocking and shoe many years ago, and decided to return it yesterday." Donna Elaina looked at Lillianna in astonishment. "That would not explain the leg changing size, or the tears, or any other phenomena related to her. You of all people must believe that!"

"You are right my dear one. It's just that as a prospective lawyer, I have been trained to look for facts and sometimes I blur the surreal with the real. In this case Princess

Camille has been looking over me, as you say like a mother. By the way, I don't know if ever I told you, but Camille was my mother's name, and I cannot deny that I have been protected all these years and events have always turned in my favor since that fateful day when I found her in the refuse pile. There is strong evidence to support the fact that she has guided me all along. It was through her that I have this really beautiful new leg, one that I can live with; also thanks to the extreme generosity of your father. Finally it is through her that I have found a friend in you. You probably didn't know this, but you were a great influence on me. I was impressed by the way you spoke when first I met you. From you I was able to see the importance of a good education. I found you, so cultured, and I so inadequate, that I was determined to improve myself and not let anything stand in the way of my success."

Donna Elaina nodded her head in disbelief. "Lillianna, you are so much more worthy than me. I mean all this stuff has been handed to me on a plate. I am the lucky one to have been born in such extraordinary circumstances!" They moved close to the doll and put their arms around her and each other. A lesser person might have thought that Princess Camille had a smile on her face.

Victor Emanuel entered the room, and stopped, allowing the door to close slowly behind him. Lillianna breathed in quickly through her nose holding her jaw tightly closed. She needed time to gather her composure. Fortunately she got it, as Donna Elaina caught sight of her brother.

"Victor, do you know whom this is?" she said, with half a smile on her face.

"No, but I certainly wish that I did!" He was self assured, and felt at ease in the company of women. He was mature and better looking than Lillianna had remembered. She walked towards him in a slow easy gait and held out her hand.

"Victor Emanuelle, it must be all of ten years since I last saw you, but I, on the contrary, would have recognized you anywhere." Victor Emanuel held her hand briefly.

"Ten years is a long time, you surely would have been a baby then. That is why I don't recognize you, though your eyes have something familiar about them."

"I'm the little girl who came here for a prosthesis."

Victor Emanuel stepped back and shook his head. "This can't be. I saw you walk across the room. You have two beautiful legs!" He flushed with embarrassment. "What I err... meant to say was that, I happened to notice your legs and couldn't see any difference, one from the other. It is truly incredible!" This was a sublime moment for Lillianna. She had certainly fooled one of the most eligible bachelors in the city. She felt supremely confident now and could move forward.

"You are Lillianna and you have a very beautiful sister called Vivienne, am I right?"

"Yes you are right on both counts." "I expect that Vivienne is now married with several children. I have so often thought about her over the years, she was so very special."

"No Victor, she has not married, and she is more beautiful than ever."

Victor Emanuel's eyes widened and a smile appeared upon his face "Then I still have a chance to correct the error I made so many years ago."

"Yes Victor you still may have a chance." Victor Emanuel straightened his tie and pulled himself erect.

"So what brings you to our home Lillianna?"

"I came to see Donna Elaina. We are becoming very close friends."

Donna Elaina came forward and put her arm around Lillianna. "Dear brother, Lillianna is starting her second year of law at our University; she is a top student there. She is head of the student body and I predict that she will be famous one day."

"Donna Elaina, you are most generous, but I fear given to exaggeration. Victor; May I call you Victor?" she said smiling.

"I would be most honored!" he was looking at her but his thoughts appeared to be elsewhere.

"Victor, what news do you have of General Armaldo?" Victor Emanuel motioned for them to sit down on the chairs, which they did. He remained standing, and moved towards the window, clasping his hands behind his back.

"I hear that he is gaining ground and that a lot of our military are going over to his side. I think that there will be a revolution soon. One of our chauffeurs recently left without notice to join his cause. My parents are quite distressed."

"I'm sad to hear about that. I owe your family a debt of gratitude; you have been so good to me. What happened to Enrico?"

Victor Emanuel smiled. He returned to the ladies. "He married a woman from your village, a childhood sweetheart apparently. He bought a home in an estate near you. He was a wonderful man and a loyal servant. I wish him great happiness and a long life. Unfortunately, his wife died a few years ago, and so his step daughter who never married, and who had lived with them at the house, looks after him. I hear that she is completely devoted to him"

Lillianna looked at her watch. "I am so happy to hear that; he is such a special man! "Oh my goodness, I must go, I have someone waiting for me at the main gate."

"Please don't go!" Victor Emanuel almost blurted it out. "I thought that you would spend the day with us. When can I… that is, when will we see you and Vivienne again? May I come and pick you up next week, next Wednesday perhaps?" He did not wish to appear anxious but was caught by the suddenness of her departure; he needed to ask more questions about Vivienne in an unhurried fashion.

"Well yes, that would be fine. I'm so sorry that I must leave now I look forward to seeing you both, next week. Goodbye." She embraced Donna Elaina. Victor Emanuel took her hands in his and kissed her on both cheeks. He walked her to the entrance on his arm.

The chauffeur who had been standing under a tree talking to a gardener rushed forward and opened the door of the limousine and Lillianna stepped inside, waving to the brother and sister on the steps. The chauffeur drove slowly down the road flanked by trees to the entrance gate. The limousine stopped and Lillianna stepped out of the car before the driver had time to run around and open the door. She waved to the driver as he slowly turned the car around and made his way back in the direction of the house. Victor Emanuel stood on the steps of the chateau peering through a pair of binoculars. He watched as a young man helped Lillianna into an old Truck.

Chapter 15

ALFREDO SAT WITH HIS ears glued to the radio, as Maria and Anita came into the room with the evening meal that they had been preparing in the kitchen. He was clearly worried by the reports of heavy fighting in the mountainous region in the north, where government troops were trying to contain rebel forces loyal to General Armaldo. News of their advance was being broadcast by the government owned radio, but the word, where he worked in a machine shop on the outskirts of town, was that the General was meeting with much success as continuing numbers of peasants and defecting military soldiers were joining his ranks. If the rebels were able to win in this area, nothing would stand in their way on their march south towards the capital.

Pedro had left two days earlier and returned to his work north of the city. He had told his parents that if things appeared to be getting worse, he would jump in his truck, go and pick Vivienne up, and come home. It was a tense time for all. Lillianna came in from the kitchen with a large bowl of rice. "What is the latest news?" she said anxiously.

Maria came to take the bowl from her. "It's difficult to say my precious. The government will only tell us what they want us to hear. We will have to wait and see." Alfredo turned the radio off and they took their seats around the table. In the prayers that followed, special mention was made for the safety of Vivienne and Pedro.

Wednesday came, and Lillianna rose early, bathed herself and put on one of the dresses that Vivienne had left at the house. It was a little shorter than she was accustomed to as Vivienne was shorter, and Lillianna felt uncomfortable showing too much of her leg. However as she stood in front of the mirror, moving from side to side to make her dress swish around her legs, she found that it didn't reveal too much. The prosthesis was very good and so much better than she could have dreamed of without the generosity of the Di Caprio family, who had insisted on paying for it. She dabbed a little perfume behind each ear from a small sample bottle that Vivienne had brought home from the store. Her hair hung loosely about her shoulders and she had borrowed a set of earrings that she particularly liked from Vivienne's jewellery box. She smiled, revealing a beautiful set of white teeth. She had no lipstick but her lips were red and full and she had no need of it.

The door bell rang and Lillianna walked swiftly along the corridor to the main room. Victor Emanuel was standing alone at the door. "Where is Donna Elaina?" she said anxiously looking beyond his shoulder. In the unpaved street at the foot of the stairs, a large shiny black car was parked with no chauffeur present. "Have you come alone?" She was alarmed at the thought of suddenly being alone with Victor Emanuel and he could see it on her face.

"May I come in." he said, gesturing toward the open door.

"Oh yes, forgive me my rudeness. Please come in!"

Victor Emanuel bowed his head as he passed through the entrance; his head barely cleared the door opening. He had his mother's good looks, and unlike his father, was very slim. Maria entered the room and he bowed his head in her direction. He turned towards Lillianna. "Several things have happened since last I saw you, although it has only been about a week. Some of our staff has left, including a personal maid of Donna Elaina's. She took Paola, Donna Elaina's doll with her. Why? I don't know, but I suspect that she did not like Donna very much, or had some bad dealings with her and took it for revenge. She ran away with the chauffeur. He was the one who drove you to our home. That's two in a row. He had only been in our employ for about a year and had seemed quite acceptable. They left a note saying that they had gone to join General Armaldo's staff, and advised others to do the same. I came here because I was concerned for your safety Lillianna. We had an appointment, but I do not think that it would be advisable for you to visit us at this time. I simply had to come and see you as there was no other way for me to communicate with you."

Lillianna saw the concern in his eyes and her heart started to beat a little faster. "My dear Victor, it was so courageous of you to come and see me, especially in light of what you have told me. Now it is I who am concerned with your safety and those of your family. I must come with you now to see Donna Elaina; she must be so afraid."

Lillianna stood up and Victor Emanuel rose with her and clasped her hands in his, looking down into her eyes. "I am sorry," he said, "I cannot permit that. You see conditions are a little worse than those stated on the radio. We have been told by our advisers to leave the country as soon as possible if we wish to guarantee our safety. It is not good to be living in a large house at this time. My father intends to remain though, and I shall stay by his side."

He kissed Lillianna on both cheeks and walked towards the door before she could utter any objections to his plan.

Lillianna followed closely behind Victor Emanuel to the door and was amazed to see Pedro drive up in his truck with Vivienne at his side. He climbed out of the truck and took the steps two at a time up to the entrance. The two men faced each other for a moment before Victor Emanuel smiling broadly, stuck out his hand. The two men shook hands. Though they were similar in height and build, the comparison ended there. Pedro's hands, large and rough almost engulfed those of Victor Emanuel. Victor Emanuel stood erect with his shoulders back, his face soft and refined. His trousers smartly pressed hung down over shiny brown leather shoes. Pedro was hunched over; his head bent forward like a man about to spring. His face wore the marks of a man who worked outdoors. His clothing was rough, but practical, he was wearing boots that were worn and creased.

Vivienne approached and stood facing them. Victor Emanuelle smiled in recognition. "It's Vivienne isn't it? You have not changed at all in all these years. You are even more beautiful than I remembered." He was smiling, but appeared tense. I'm not sure how my condition will be over the next few months, and maybe it is this uncertainty which makes me act the way that I do now, but if all ends well, I would consider it a great honor if you would permit me to visit you!"

Vivienne moved backwards and put her hands behind her against the wall. She was shaken but managed to regain her composure. Here was a man who would have no problem finding eligible ladies in his circle of friends, but who was asking permission to visit her. She closed her eyes and breathed slowly through her nostrils. She felt dizzy and wanted to sit down. A voice came from within her.

"I am so surprised to see you here Victor Emanuel. My brother, who works farther north, heard the rumble of approaching artillery, he and his fellow workers decided to leave. He drove south at high speed to my place of work, and picked me up". She looked lovingly at her brother. "The stores are starting to close now and shop owners are putting boards over the windows. Soon the roads will be crowded so it is I who am concerned for you."

Victor Emanuel moved closer to her "I am touched that you should be concerned for my safety Vivienne. There is no need though I do assure you."

Vivienne could scarcely breathe but she knew that this was not the moment to lack courage. She walked towards him and placed her hand on his arm. "Victor, we shall look forward to seeing you when all this is over, but our concern now is that you leave 'post haste' before the routes become impassible."

"Yes, I should return now, but I go with the thought that I will see you very soon. Please take care, all of you!" He placed a foot on the top stair, turned, peering into the faces of the three of them for one last time. Slowly he descended the stairs, one at a time and entered his car. He did not look back. They stood, Pedro in the center, with his arms around the girls, looking at the car until it passed out of sight.

Chapter 16

.....General Armaldo's staff car moved out from behind two large tanks and glided over the bumpy road to within fifty meters of the crest of the hill. Here it stopped and the driver got out and ran around to the side of the car and opened the door. He stood stiffly to attention and saluted as the general stepped out onto the road, followed by two of his senior staff officers. His aide, Captain Alphonse di Mourni Del Castieza, a fat little man with a short manicured moustache, whose role in life was to satisfy the General's every whim, moved out cautiously from the front seat next to the driver. He pushed the door open slowly and stood behind it as he glanced to his left and ahead of him to where the general stood.

The General had his eyes fixed upon two scouts who had been sent forward and were now crouched down waving for him to come up to the front to assess the situation. The General walked forward followed by his two subordinates, his bearing every inch that of a military man. He bent low and removed his hat, as he moved, crouched in a half run towards the summit. Once at the crest and positioned next to one of the scouts, he lay down on his stomach and fumbled in his right coat pocket for his binoculars. He pulled them out, almost automatically, as he scanned the road below. It was completely clear of traffic and indeed all signs of life.

To the left of the road, a narrow stand of trees and brush, about one kilometer wide, stretched along the entire left side off the road into the distant hills; an ideal hiding place for a small platoon with tanks. He swept the area with his binoculars focusing on the road ahead. It went down into a valley before rising and passing between two mountains in the distance. It was here in this pass and on the sides of the mountains that government force were massed some five kilometers away. Here, they would make their stand, the last obstruction before the city some twenty kilometers ahead. Driving down the hill into the jaws of the enemy would be an invitation to suicide. Even if they were to succeed, the road passed through a long stretch of jungle before arriving at the city.

The General turned toward his subordinates. "Gentlemen, at first light, we will turn our guns on this stand of trees to see if there are any surprises awaiting us. Then we will send out a scouting party to see what we have uncovered. In short, we will use every conceivable ploy to encourage the enemy into thinking that we are preparing for a full frontal attack. In the mean time I want each of you to take two platoons and encircle the enemy from both sides and cut them off from the rear." His eyes darted from one to the other of his subalterns, who could only look at him in dumb amazement. He continued. "Now I know that this is difficult terrain and it will take several days to cut our way through this dense jungle area, but time is our enemy, and speed is of utmost importance. When this is accomplished we will drive down the road with our tanks and confront the enemy. I would like to wish you the very best of luck! Are there any questions?"

One of the officers, a small man very much overweight, with a walrus moustache, stepped forward. "Sir I question the need of sending two platoons in opposite directions to encircle the enemy. Wouldn't it be better if the two platoons went along the same path, and spread out in the rear behind the enemy?"

"I appreciate your comment Ernst, said the General pulling on his white moustache which spread to the edges of his face, "but this terrain is unfamiliar to us and our maps are poor. We may encounter rocky escarpments or ravines on one side which would hold us up for days. It is my hope that one platoon will make it through and start the attack from the rear within forty eight hours, that is why I am sending you off in two different directions."

The officers looked at each other in silence, but made no comment. The General continued. "The other platoon on hearing the sound of gunfire should turn east, or west, as the case may be, and head for the road attacking from the side. I shall remain here and give every indication that I'm regrouping and staffing up for a frontal attack. Thank you gentlemen and good luck!"

The two officers stood to attention and saluted the General. They turned on their heels and walked off leaving the general focusing his binoculars on the route ahead. Behind him the sound of heavy machinery could be heard as big guns were being brought up the hill from the rear.

Captain Antonio Hernandez was in his tent writing down the events of the day, when an orderly opened the flap. "Excuse me my Captain. The General Armaldo wishes to see you in his tent at your earliest convenience.

The Captain sprang up from his seat and reached for his jacket. He was tall and lean. His thick wavy hair was parted on the left hand side and had been brought under control by some kind of gel. His hair at the back was short, military style. He buttoned his jacket and threw his gun belt around his waist and buckled it up. He adjusted his hat in the mirror and walked out from under his tent flap into the warm evening air. The general's tent was across an open stretch of ground almost opposite. He walked swiftly in the direction of the tent as a thousand thoughts passed through his mind.

At the marquee two sentries posted each side of the entrance sprang to attention and saluted the Captain as he entered. The general was standing with his arms clasped behind him looking at the floor.

He looked up. "Ah. Hernandez!" he said, as the Captain sprung to attention and saluted. "I have an important mission for you." He motioned for the Captain to follow him to a large table, where several senior staff officers were assembled. "Captain," he said, gesturing with his hand for him to join the group at the table. "Captain, tomorrow at first light we will commence bombing this forest with our heavy artillery." He pointed to a map that a cartographer had drawn up. A forest lined the route on the east side of the road heading south into the city. The Captain was familiar with the area having gone out two weeks earlier on a scouting mission after dark, when he encountered nothing. "Directly after the attack I want you to take a scouting party into the area to see if there are any significant signs of the enemy. Take half a dozen men with you and report back your findings. The enemy could have laid mines or traps of some kind so be aware of that."

"Yes my Genera!."

"That will be all Captain you may retire to your quarters!"

The General turned and moved in amongst his men with his aide a few steps behind him. "Personally I don't think he will find anything there." he said. "The only route is in the valley between the two mountains on that road. They are probably well dug in there so have no need of protection from the forest, but just to be sure I shall have my Captain reconnoiter. He is a fine young man and I know that he will do a thorough job."

There was a pause in the conversation. He looked down at his feet placing his hands once more behind his back before speaking. "Gentlemen, I have good news. My intelligence reports that, in a surprise attack during the night on the two enemy air force bases, our commando's have taken prisoner of all but four of the air force pilots, with no loss of lives. There will be no air war here!" A loud cheer went up from the Señor staff. "Over the next forty eight hours we are going to simulate a heavy build up of machinery this end. We must do everything in our power to let the enemy know that an attack is immanent. I am hoping for a mass defection to our side, and would like to minimize loss of lives on both sides. The government forces are making their last stand here. If we can smash through their defenses at the end of this road, then the capital is ours!" Another cheer from the staff prompted the general to raise his hands. "Now gentlemen let us get some sleep. We have a busy day tomorrow."

The shelling began at six fifteen and lasted for more than an hour. Whole trees were flung up into the air as heavy guns systematically bombed the forest on the left side of the road. They were calculated to land about fifty feet apart, staring at a point over three kilometers away and move rearward closer to their source. Only the large guns could be seen on the top of the hill. All other tanks and heavy artillery had been removed to a safe distance from them to avoid being targeted by the enemy. But there was no sound from the enemy during this eerie silence that followed the bombing,

Captain Hernandez and his patrol moved out to search the forest. Huge craters scarred the land and uprooted trees lay facing out from each center like so many hands on a clock. It soon became evident to the Captain that there was no advanced guard or any kind of defensive forces dug in along the three kilometer stretch. However he decided to continue right up to the end. Progress was slow as at each crater center, it was necessary to skirt the area in order to save time. He had split his force into two sections, each one circling the craters from opposite sides and joining in the middle before moving to the next crater.

At some point during this process when they had gone about a mile, a sergeant from the other group motioned to the Captain for him to join him. He and his group moved silently around the crater and joined the sergeant on the other side. There behind a fallen tree lay two people, a man and a women laying face down, dressed in servants attire. They were quite obviously dead and had bullet wounds in their backs. They wore arm bands depicting the colors of General Armaldo's forces, green orange and red. Captain Hernandez kneeled down between the bodies and put his hand on the woman's neck. He looked up at the sergeant. She is still warm!" he whispered with astonishment. It was at this moment that he saw some movement in the brush ahead. "Take cover, men!" he yelled, at the same time diving sideways over the body of the man to a depression behind a clump of trees. He heard the wine of a bullet and felt a sharp pain in his left arm. His bone had been shattered above the elbow, and he cried out in pain. The sergeant sprang into action. He directed his men to fan out, and they moved swiftly forward each protecting the other with short bursts of fire as they ran from tree to tree.

Quite suddenly, three men stood up with their hands above their heads. They looked very scared. The Sergeant motioned for them to approach him while three riflemen had their sights trained upon them. The others, hidden by thick brush scanned the area for possible signs of any movement ahead of them. Captain Hernandez stood up and held his left arm. He was in terrible pain, but managed to gain control of the situation.

"Take these men prisoners Sergeant and march them to the road!" It was then that he lost consciousness, and fell to the ground. The medic attached to the group ran to his side and applied a tourniquet to his arm above the wound. He then set about bandaging the shattered arm using splints to keep the bones from doing more damage. He placed his Captain's arm in a sling, and gave him an injection of morphine.

Slowly the Captain regained consciousness. His eyes were watery and out of focus, and he closed them several times to try to regain a clear vision. He began to think that he was dreaming because he had this phantom like image of a beautiful woman with flaxen hair standing some way off before him. With his good hand he rubbed his eyes, and looked again; slowly they came into focus. What he saw was not an illusion at all, but a beautiful large doll dressed in fine white silk and lace. It was standing upright in between some bushes and appeared to be smiling at him. Captain Hernandez propped himself up into the upright position. Slowly, he eased himself over to where the doll stood and with his good hand drew it to him. One of his men came towards him and helped him to his feet. He was feeling dizzy and in great pain, and he passed the doll to one of his subordinates, telling him to hold onto it, as it would serve in identifying the two patriots who had died coming to join them. He assembled his men and started the long treck over fallen trees towards the road. Away from the blast center going became easier and eventually they found a track heading in the right direction, heading westward. The men were strung out behind him with the prisoners, their hands bound behind them, in the rear.

Half an hour later they were in sight of the road. They could hear distant muffled sounds, but in no way could they make sense of them nor the direction from whence they came. Finally the Captain struggled up the rise to the road followed by his men and the prisoners. What he saw next amazed him. Coming up from the south were thousands upon thousands of soldiers waving white flags and cheering as they strolled towards the army of General Armaldo massed upon the hill. What a sight the Captain must have presented to them. He had his arm in a sling, one of his men stood beside him carrying a large doll, and behind them, three prisoners in government army uniforms, their hands tied behind their backs followed by more men wearing the uniform of the rebel army

The General leading the cheering soldiers called a halt to the procession and stopped in front of the Captain. He saluted and presented his sword to him. He then officially surrendered his entire army to the Captain. General Armaldo watched the event through his binoculars as Captain Hernandez took the sword and waving it above his head, moved to the front of the column and led the long procession up the hill. Twenty minutes later he arrived. Pain and exhaustion had left him in the euphoria of the moment, one that he would remember for the rest of his life. He presented the sword to the General and handed over the entire government forces to him. A huge roar went up from both sides of the conflict. The war was at a close.

Chapter 17

Two weeks had gone by with no sound of the war. Radio silence had been maintained throughout, with the exception of music, which was transmitted for two hours every day. Alfredo had been obliged to kill two of his layer chickens and dig into his supply of root crops that he had stored in his shed. One day he cycled to his old village to see if there was any news. They were in a worse situation than he. The dumpster trucks from town had stopped, so food had become very scarce there.

Finally the news that all had hoped for, but could scarcely believe, broke. The military under General Armaldo had taken control of the government. The radio station, water supply, banks and power stations, road and rail services and the international airport were in the hands of the military. Corrupt government officials including the President had flown into exile. Resistance had been weak; it had been a bloodless coup.

General Armaldo has requested that everyone stay calm, and return to his or her place of work as soon as possible. He stated, that he was a soldier, loyal to his country, and it was not his intention to enter into politics or stay as head of government, but that he would remain in that position until a year from now when democratically held elections would take place. He went on to say that International Aid had been promised; that the International Airport had been reopened to foreign traffic, also that fact finding missions from foreign countries were either in place or would be arriving within the next day or so.

It was Friday and the busses were running. Vivienne returned from the Police station on the outskirts of the city. She had gone there to make a phone call to her department store to find out when they would be open for business. To her surprise they had told her that although the store would not be open for two weeks, she was on the list of names of staff that they would like to see as early as Monday to assist in preparation for reopening. She was feeling happy at the idea that she had been chosen among the few who would be given the responsibility for the stores reopening. She could get back to helping her family financially, and enjoy the sometime boring rhythm of a normal life. She was met at the door by Pedro. "I am going to start again Monday, I can hardly believe it. We have the General Armaldo to thank for this."

Lillianna entered the room. She had washed and dressed, and she walked over to Pedro and kissed him on both cheeks.

"Vivienne, I didn't hear you get up this morning, you were so quiet." Pedro put his arm on Lillianna's shoulder.

"Guess what little 'sis' Vivienne is going back to work Monday. That means that the roads are clear and so I will drive her in, and go and see if we have opened up for work."

"No thanks Pedro." said Vivienne. "I know that you will want an early start to go north. I shall take the bus into town. It stops right outside our store."

Lillianna put her hand on Pedro's shoulder. "I would like to go with you Pedro if you don't mind. I am very concerned about the well being of Donna Elaina. It's not good to be living in a mansion during these times of turmoil."

Pedro smiled his teeth so white against his dark brown skin. "Are you sure that you are not more worried about a certain Victor Emanuel also." Lillianna blushed. "I am worried about the whole family, but in particular Donna Elaina, she does not have the stoicism or courage of the others."

"Stoicism! What is this word? Lillianna, with all this education you are slowly leaving me behind."

Lillianna threw her arms around Pedro's neck and hugged him. "Never!" she said.

Lillianna arrived in front of the mansion of the Di Caprio family. She was very relieved to see that the gates had not been breeched, and that the same old man came out from his lodge to greet her. She turned to Pedro and kissed him on his cheek. "Thank you big brother, I will be able to get home from here, and I will phone Vivienne at the store to let her know how things are."

Pedro appeared to be a little sad. "I will come and see you soon. Now go, and don't say hello to Victor Emanuel for me."

Lillianna turned quickly towards him. "You are forgetting my dear brother that he only has eyes for Vivienne." She got out of the truck and he sped off, his wheels skidding as he drove around the bend out of sight.

The old man opened the gate. "Please come in Madame. I will announce your presence to Miss Di Caprio."

Shortly thereafter a limo could be seen leaving the Mansion coming slowly down the long driveway in the shade of a long line of trees. It arrived at the gate and Victor Emanuel jumped out and ran to her and kissed her on the cheek. Lillianna was startled by his sudden show of affection. "I am so happy to see you, and how is your sister Vivienne, and of course your family? "

"Vivienne is fine and my family is greatly relieved that the war is over." said Lillianna smiling broadly

The chauffeur opened the door and Donna Elaina descended and stood waiting near the front of the car. Lillianna ran towards her.

"Donna! I was so worried about you, and I cannot express how happy I am to see you." They embraced.

"I am happy to see you also Lillianna. My brother and I are on our way to the war memorial in the center of the city. My father is already there along with some city elders to receive this brutish upstart General to try and accommodate him under the new régime. Please say that you will come with us! We can talk on the way."

Lillianna thought for a second before replying. "I would love to go; but what good timing! A little later and I would have missed you," Lillianna walked with them back to the car where the chauffeur was waiting by the door. "Oh, I've just remembered something, May I use the phone at the gate? I promised my sister that I would call her."

"Your sister?" asked Victor Emanuel. "You mean Vivienne?"

"Yes Vivienne, she is working in town."

"I do not think that she will be now. We just heard on the radio, that all the stores are closing and today has been proclaimed a National Holiday." said a joyful Victor Emanuel. "Tell her that we will come to pick her up."

Lillianna phoned her sister, and after some persuasion got her to leave her place of work and come with the Di Caprio family to the town square where the General would be addressing the country.

Victor Emanuel walked over to the chauffeur who was standing by the rear door of the limousine, to give him instructions on where to find the department store in town. The chauffeur politely assured him that he was familiar with the department store as he had driven Miss Donna Elaina there on several occasions. The three of them entered the limousine and Victor Emanuel pulled down a rearward facing seat in front of the ladies. The chauffeur closed the door and took his place behind the wheel. He nodded to the Gatekeeper and they glided out onto the boulevard leading to town.

Chapter 18

General Armaldo's entourage had stopped in front of Plaza de los Muertos, a large plaza with an obelisk in the center of town, where a throng of many thousands had gathered to hear his address. Several dignities, including Señor Di Caprio, were standing each side of the monument at the foot of the stairs, where the General had come to lay a wreath. Behind him, members of his senior staff were getting out of a long line of vehicles. Military police with rifles and fixed bayonets were in place ready to hold the crowd back should the need arise. Men in civilian clothing were positioned in the crowd to be ready for any possible attack by a lunatic or fanatic to the old regime. The crowd was cheering loudly and waving the national flag. In one of the staff cars, a young Captain in uniform with his arm in a sling was being assisted out onto the street, by one of his men. The car was open at the back, and on the rear seat sat a doll with flaxen hair.

General Armaldo walked to his dais facing the throng, while the other dignitaries took their seat in the first two rows. He opened his speech by declaring that although the country was under military rule at this time, he had no desire to stay as head of state and that democratic elections would be held one year from this date. Amid the cheers from the hundreds of thousands of spectators he spoke of the need to press for education for every child in the country; of installing government schools in even the remotest villages and to have a government run health facility to oversee the nutritional and health needs of children from birth to adulthood. "These are our children and the future of our country," he said his voice rising to avoid being drowned out by the cheers from the crowd

Donna Elaina strode forward followed by Victor Emanuel, with Vivienne and Lillianna close behind. They took seats in the third row behind some government officials. Donna Elaina waved to her father who was in the front row further down. Behind them sat rows of senior military officers and their families. She groaned, and whispered to her brother that the General appeared to have communistic leanings, and that they would no longer be able to afford their household staff. Victor smiled and motioned for her to keep quiet. She looked aimlessly at the faces of the military men behind the General and her gaze wandered to the road and to the military drivers standing beside the staff cars. Her eyes caught sight of what appeared to be a little girl in the rear seat of one of the cars. She squinted, trying to bring her eyes into focus, and cupped her hand over her brow to avoid the suns glare. Then she stood up and started to walk to the end of the row of empty seats next to her; her hand still shielding her eyes. She turned and walked in front of the first row of officials, her pace quickened. Heads turned as she started to run towards the staff cars, one hand holding onto the hat on her head. "My baby! My baby!" she cried as all heads including the General's turned to follow her. She stopped at the side of the car where Princess Camille was seated. The driver, wide eyed at the sight of this somewhat plump symbol of the ruling class descending upon him at high speed, looked to his Captain, who was already on his way to his car. The driver walked forward gallantly to bar her from reaching the car, but he was no match for her as she swung him around and pushed him out of the way.

The Captain had by this time arrived at the car, and took her firmly by the arm bringing her to a standstill. She looked up at this handsome man with his left arm in a sling, and smiled coyly at him.

"Is this your staff car Captain?" she said brushing her hair back under her hat.

"Yes Mademoiselle, it is." Her tone had softened and she regained some of her composure.

"Well Sire; that is my doll which you have in your car, and I would like to know how you came by it!" The Captain relaxed his grip upon her arm and smiled triumphantly.

"I would be most happy to return your doll to you later, but first there are some questions that I must ask. This I will do when the General has finished his speech." He offered his arm to her. "May I have the pleasure of escorting you back to your seat Madame?" Donna Elaina smiled coyly at him, fluttering her eyelids as she spoke.

"Yes Sir you may!" She put her arm in his and he escorted her back to her seat. As he arrived his gaze rested upon Lillianna. He appeared to be transfixed. He had never seen someone as beautiful as her in his entire life. He looked at Victor Emanuel, who was whispering something to Vivienne. He was relieved to see him holding her hand. He nodded, and bowed his head to the ladies, and looked once more at Lillianna before returning to his place behind the dais.

The General looked slowly to his left and then to his right to see if there would be any further disturbance. He was frowning and he lowered his head looking out at the crowd under his white bushy eyebrows. He continued his speech. Some fifteen minutes later he concluded by saying that although the war had been somewhat limited and could have been far worse; there had been unfortunately causalities on both sides of the conflict. He raised his hands and opened them towards the crowd. "My heart goes out to the families who have lost their loved ones in this struggle. Each, in his or her own way, believed firmly in this cause. I can only tell you that I will do my best in the year ahead to help the aggrieved and suffering; to try to heal their wounds, and not to forget what these patriots gave up for the betterment of this country." He stood stiffly to attention, saluted, and said. "My fellow countrymen I salute you all. "God bless our Country!".There was a loud roar of approval from the hundreds of thousands as they waved and blew horns. The guests seated, rose and clapped while the military men saluted him. Lillianna rose and clapped loudly.

"What a wonderful, wonderful man this General is she said, leaning and turning towards Donna Elaina.

"Equality is never a good thing!" was her forthright reply.

Captain Hernandez lost no time in returning to where Donna Elaina was seated; his driver carrying the doll, close behind him. "I am most happy to return your doll to you Madame." he said to Donna Elaina, though his eyes never left those of Lillianna. "The reason that I brought this doll here with me in the first place, was because I was hoping that someone in the crowd would recognize it, and that we could find out more about the couple who had it in their possession when they were killed."

"When they were killed?" said Donna Elaina who was busy looking her doll over to see if all her parts were there. "Did the man have a chauffeur's uniform on, and the women a maid's attire?"

"Yes Madame, that is correct. They were young, perhaps in their mid thirties."

"That sounds like Alfonso and Marguerite." She kissed her doll. "They were on my father's staff and ran away during the night. She was my personal maid, but hardly compliant. The pair of them were nothing more than common thieves; I have little pity for them."

Quite suddenly the General was at their side. He was a giant of a man, and as distinguished looking as Pedro had said. "Well Captain," he said, "Did you have any luck finding who the unfortunate couple was?"

"Yes Sir, I believe we have found out more about them. They were household staff of the parents of this young lady."

"Oh that is truly wonderful," the General said. "They were true patriots, wearing our flag like a badge of honor on their arms. Now we can put a name on their graves, and give them a proper burial. Good work Captain." The General nodded to the group that had gathered, and started to wander off, his hands clasped behind his back

"Sir!" The Captain spoke, clearly startled to hear his own voice. "Sir, I would be honored to introduce you to this family." The general turned and looked with furrowed brows at the Captain.

"Err, well yes, very well Captain," he said. "That would be a pleasure." The Captain was playing for time and was anxious to know what connection if any there was between Lillianna and Victor Emanuel.

"Allow me that honor Sir." said Victor Emanuel, stepping forward. "My name is Victor Emanuel.Di Caprio and I have the honor of presenting to you my sister Donna Elaina and our friends of many years Vivienne and Lillianna Garcia" The General blinked, then stepped forward and bowed to kissed the hands of the ladies. He straightened up and shook Victor Emanuel's hand.

"Tell me Di Caprio, what is it that you do?"

"Well sir I am lawyer working in my father's company."

"Indeed, indeed, a lawyer you say?" was the reply. "Well Di Caprio I wonder if you could do me a service?"

"Please name it Sire, it would be an honor." Victor Emanuel sprung to attention forgetting for a moment that he was not in the army. The General spoke.

"Well, Di Caprio, a long time ago in the previous conflict, we were under heavy attack from the enemy; the one we have just ousted. I was separated from my family as I pulled to the rear to protect our retreat to the border. I was told that they had been killed, but never had any conformation on that. Being introduced to this young lady reminded me that I once had a daughter who was called Lillianna who would be about the same age as this young lady now. Her mother's name was Camille and..." Lillianna turned her head sharply and look into the eyes of the General. Her head began to spin and her legs felt weak. She slumped to the floor. The Captain rushed over and kneeled beside her, cupping her body in his arms. She was so beautiful; he wanted to smother her with a thousand kisses. Instead he removed the sling from his arm, picked her up and took her to the empty seats and sat with her cradled in his lap.

The General walked over his brow wrinkled. "The sun must have got to her." He said wafting his hat over her face. "Young lady," he said looking at Donna Elaina. "Would you kindly loosen her belt at the waist and try to give her some air." His senior staff, who were never very far from him, ran to his side. He put his arms out. "Give her room men. Give her room!" he said moving them back.

Donna Elaina loosened Lillianna's belt. Then she stood up, walked to the Generals side and whispered in his ear, "She too had a mother called Camille, General."

The general looked up, his white eyebrows almost covering his eyes. He stood up and said, "Oh my god! Let me take a look at her!" He ran and kneeled by her side, looking into her face, searching for what could pass for a family resemblance. Donna Elaina holding her doll straddled across her hip, bent down and pulled Lillianna's arm out from under the protective arm of the Captain. She grasped the bracelet around Lillianna's wrist.

"General," she said, "does this look at all familiar?" The General feverishly grabbed the bracelet and turned it over. He looked at it for a moment, moving it between thumb and forefinger. Tears filled his eyes.

"Would you be so kind as to read, the inscription, young lady? I appear to have a problem with my eyes at this moment."

"With great pleasure my General." said Donna Elaina, taking the bracelet once more in her hands. "The inscription reads, To C. forever my love. B." Tears flowed freely down his face now as he put his arms around his daughter.

He kept on repeating. "She's mine! She's mine!" He broke into a sob kissing her on her cheeks.

Lillianna slowly awoke from her sleep, and peering down into her eyes was Captain Antonio Hernandez. She felt a warmth rise within her and thought that she must be sleeping. Her dress had come up a little revealing her prosthesis. The Captain gently pulled it down and cupped her face in his hand. He felt a strong urge to protect her, to hold her in his arms and make her feel safe. She suddenly sat upright and saw the general kneeling at her side his face red and swollen with tears.

"Father is that really you?"

"Yes my darling girl, it is I, your father."

She reached up and embraced him covering his face with kisses and hugging him. "Mother may be gone," she said "but I am here to look after you now father. I will never leave you again!"

"Nor will I you my dear." said the General his voice croaking out the words. They stood up laughing and crying and hugging each other, as the crowd of officers who learning of the news, looked on shaking their heads in amazement. His aide, Captain Alphonse di Mourni Del Castieza called for three cheers.

Captain Hernandez picked up his hat, dusted it off, and placed it upon his head. "This is a great day!" he said, "One that all of us will remember for the rest of our lives!"

"That is true." said the General. "God grant me a few good years to be with my daughter!" Lillianna had both arms around her father. She looked over at Princess Camille, cradled in Donna Elaina's arm. She put her hand to her mouth and blew the Princess a kiss.

"It is you my Princess who have been my guardian angel all these years. People may think what they like, but I know it to be true." she whispered. Princess Camille had a few tears in her eyes. They glistened and she seemed to be smiling.

Lillianna turned to her father who was looking down upon her as if he'd found the largest and brightest of jewels in the world "Father, your name starts with a B, what is it?" The General turned his head towards the Captain Hernandez, his eyes narrowed and his bushy eyebrows became as one. Captain Hernandez sprung to attention, his neck pushed firmly into his shoulders. The General scowled a little and furrowed his brow.

"It's, err… Beauregard, my dear." The words uttered almost in a whisper.

"Father, I'm sorry, I didn't quite hear you!" The General turned again to look at his Captain.

"It's Beauregard Armaldo!"

"Beauregard Armaldo, what a wonderful name!" she said. The Captain's head shrunk further into his shoulders. He closed his eyes. His bottom lip started to twitch. If there was the hint of a smile on his face he was going to stifle it.

Chapter 19

CATHEDRAL BELLS RANG OUT as a stretched limousine pulled up in front of the entrance to the cathedral. A footman walked forward and opened the rear door. Out stepped Alfredo dressed in a grey morning suit. He was wearing a pair of black patent leather shoes and carrying a top hat in his white gloved hand. He put his hand forward and helped his daughter Vivienne out of the car. She was wearing a magnificent long white dress with a white laced bridle train. Two pages ran forward to carry her train as she mounted the steps of the Cathedral on her father's arm. The wedding march began to play as they walked down the aisle. She waved through tears as well wishers on each side of the aisle turned to look at her. Alfredo had his head held high and turned neither to the left nor right as they began the solemn walk to the altar.

Victor Emanuel turned to look upon his bride. He was smiling, but his eyes were glazed over. His brother Umberto was at his side. On one side of the aisle at the front was the Di Caprio family. Donna Elaina was sitting with Princess Camille on her lap; she had been escorted into the Church by the Captain Alphonse di Mourni, Del Castieza, who was under strict orders from the General, to satisfy her every whim. Directly behind her, next to the aisle, sat Enrico and his step daughter. He was frail now and bowed with age, but he still had a strong shock of white hair and dark doleful eyes that twinkled as he looked around him at familiar faces in the congregation. Many friends of the family and elders of the city sat next to them, and behind them and at the rear were representatives of the household staff, many of whom had known Victor Emanuel as a baby.

On the other side of the aisle sat members and friends of the Garcia family. Maria with her son Pedro and relatives of the family sat in the first row, behind them Captain Hernandez and the General, resplendent in their uniforms and behind them were rows and rows of friends from the village.

The maids of honor, Sandra, Lillianna and Anita looked beautiful in their pink gowns as they turned sideways to face the congregation. Lillianna cast her eyes down at her left hand splayed out before her. She moved it slowly and watched the diamonds sparkle and dance around the blue sapphire stone in the center of her engagement ring. She felt a warm glow from within as she looked over at the two men who would come to mean so much to her in her new life. Her Captain who was looking intently at her, smiled as her eyes met his. Her father, the General was also looking with pride at his daughter. He bowed his head and touched his hand to his lips, blowing her a kiss. She smiled and nodded her head, then turned to Donna Elaina. Donna Elaina had placed Princess Camille on her lap so that she could see the proceedings a little better. Princess Camille though, was looking directly at Lillianna. Lillianna blew her a kiss. It was Camille after all, who found her in her misery in the cave entrance next to the hill of trash. It was Camille, who ensured that she would receive a new leg. It was through Camille that she was reunited with her father, and Camille who found her future husband in the woods and led him to her. Could it really be that Lillianna's mother was watching over her after all, through Camille? From where Lillianna stood at the foot of the altar, in the flickering candlelight, Camille appeared to be smiling...........

Printed in the United States
124747LV00003B/23/A

9 781587 368431